BACK
IN ACTION

BACK
IN ACTION

Elvira Woodruff

DRAWINGS BY

Will Hillenbrand

HOLIDAY HOUSE / NEW YORK

Text copyright © 1991 by Elvira Woodruff
Illustrations copyright © 1991 by Will Hillenbrand
ALL RIGHTS RESERVED
Printed in the United States of America
FIRST EDITION

Library of Congress Cataloging-in-Publication Data
Woodruff, Elvira.
Back in action / by Elvira Woodruff ; pictures by Will
Hillenbrand.
p.   cm.
Summary: After finding the magic powder again, Noah and his friend
Nate shrink to the size of Noah's miniature toy men and have an
exciting adventure.
ISBN 0-8234-0897-3
[1. Magic—Fiction.   2. Size—Fiction.   3. Toys—Fiction.]
I. Hillenbrand, Will, ill.   II. Title.
PZ7.W8606Bac   1991   91-2093   CIP   AC
[Fic]—dc20

c. 1   1993   PF ©

*For the original
little Jack Carlton,
with love*

E. W.

*For my brothers,
Bob and Pete,
in memory of Rick*

W. H.

BACK
IN ACTION

CHAPTER ONE

"Help, Commander! I'm heading straight for the oatmeal pit!" Noah Murphy whispered in his goofy Gordy voice. It was Saturday morning at the Murphy house and everyone was sitting at the kitchen table eating breakfast.

Noah had brought his two favorite toy men, Gordy and the Commander, to the table. For years, he had been collecting tiny plastic action figures and storing them in shoe boxes under his bed. The Commander and his sidekick Sergeant Gordy were Noah's favorites, and he rarely went anywhere without them. Gordy had a goofy gap-toothed grin and a head of wavy red hair. On

3

Noah's make-believe adventures, Gordy always got into mischief. The Commander, on the other hand, was serious. He looked strong, with a square jaw and a thick brown mustache. He was Noah's hero in all their games, since the Commander led the rescue missions and braved all danger.

Noah's family was accustomed to seeing Noah's "little guys" all over the house. They had also gotten used to hearing Noah act out his different adventures in strange little voices.

This Saturday morning Noah had tied a piece of string from the sugar bowl to the top of his chair. He pretended it was a rope ladder for Gordy and the Commander. They were on a special mission, and Gordy was about to lose his balance. Noah opened his hand, and watched the little plastic figure plummet down into his bowl of oatmeal. Globs of the cereal flew out of the bowl and landed on the table. Noah quickly looked up to see if anyone had noticed.

Noah's eight-year-old brother, Jess, was sitting beside him. Jess hadn't seen anything, because he had been too busy flattening his nose with his spoon. He was trying to make his little cousin Jack laugh. Jack was sitting across the table in a high chair. He was staying with the Murphys for the weekend while his parents were at a wedding. Jack was only two years old, and he would laugh at just about anything. He hooted with laughter at the sight of Jess pressing the spoon to his nose.

"Oh, Jess, now look what you've got him doing," Mrs. Murphy scolded. Everyone stared at Jack, who was trying to flatten the nose of his toy monster, AckAck.

"That is the ugliest toy I've ever seen." Mrs. Murphy winced as she looked at the plastic creature sitting beside her nephew in his high chair. "I can't imagine what your father was thinking when he bought you that thing."

It was true, AckAck was an exceptionally ugly toy. He seemed to be a combination dinosaur and comic book creature, standing on two legs. He had a long neck like a brontosaurus and fangs like a werewolf. Bright red blood was painted on his skin to look like it was dripping from his mouth and down his neck.

"Why do you think Jack calls him Ack-Ack?" Jess asked, as he watched Jack trying to put a piece of toast into AckAck's mouth.

"I bet he wanted to name his monster after himself," Noah said. "He probably couldn't say the J part so instead of coming out Jack, it came out Ack and then AckAck."

"That's not a bad theory, Noah." Mr. Murphy smiled.

"I can't imagine how a two-year-old could want to take that thing to bed with him at night," Mrs. Murphy said, shaking her head.

"Jack is not your normal two-year-old, Mom," Jess pointed out. "Jack is a monster lover. Do you remember the time Grandma gave him that cute little stuffed bunny for Easter? He threw it on the barbecue when Uncle Mark was cooking burgers."

"Face it, the kid just hates cute," Noah laughed.

"He's such a cutie himself, though," Mrs. Murphy said, cutting up some banana slices and putting them on Jack's tray.

Mom is right, Noah was thinking, as he looked at his little cousin's chubby cheeks and copper-colored curls. Mrs. Murphy leaned over and gave Jack a kiss. Noah silently placed his spoon over Gordy, who was now submerged in the oatmeal.

"It's a good thing you're wearing your air packs on this mission," Noah whispered, as Gordy's tiny hand sank under the oatmeal. Although Mrs. Murphy hadn't seen Gordy's fall, it was only a matter of time before she discovered the accident. Mrs. Murphy was just that kind of mother.

She notices things that only Sherlock Holmes would notice, Noah was thinking. Just yesterday Mrs. Murphy had sent Noah to the bathroom to brush his teeth. He had spent fifteen minutes playing with the toothpaste instead, making little alien toothpaste globs for his guys to attack. When he came down, Mrs. Murphy had taken one look at him and noticed that his lips were "too dry for someone who has just brushed his teeth." She had sent him back up to "brush again." She had also noticed a little toothpaste on Noah's shirt and deduced that he must have been playing with it. "And please clean up the sink before you come down again," she added.

"My goodness, watching Jack is a full-time job," Mrs. Murphy said now as she cleaned up some cereal that Jack had thrown on the floor. Jack was happily banging his spoon on the tray of the high chair.

Noah smiled and looked down into his bowl. Maybe with Jack here, Mom won't be noticing so many things, he thought happily, spooning some oatmeal over Gordy's head as it popped up.

"Glop, glop, glop, get me out of here." Noah had begun whispering again in his goofy Gordy voice. "Why couldn't you have had something good for breakfast, like pancakes? Now that would be a dish I would gladly dive into!" Noah reached for the Commander and held him over the bowl.

"Come now, Gordy, courage. Don't you know that oatmeal is the breakfast of champions?" Noah whispered in his deep Commander voice.

"Glop glop glop . . . Champions?" Noah had switched back to his Gordy voice. "I think you've got the wrong breakfast, Commander. From where I'm sitting it looks like the breakfast of . . ."

"Did you say something, Noah?" Mr. Murphy looked up from his morning paper.

"Uh . . . No, Dad. I was just playing with my guys," Noah replied, switching back to his own voice.

Mr. Murphy looked directly at Gordy, who had bounced to the surface of Noah's oatmeal.

"You and your guys," Mr. Murphy sighed, returning his attention to his newspaper. Unlike his wife, Mr. Murphy never seemed to notice anything at all. He was a tall, gangly man with reddish-brown hair and a mustache. His hair was the same color as Noah's, except that Mr. Murphy's hairline was receding and what hair he had was on the long

side, wiry and kind of crazy looking, as if it
had just exploded out of his head. Mrs. Murphy's hair, on the other hand, sat in short
orderly blond waves on her head. As she
turned to look at Noah, he pushed Gordy
down with his spoon and stared off into
space.

"Noah, you've hardly touched your oatmeal," Mrs. Murphy said. "You'll never
grow up to be big and strong if you don't eat
a good breakfast. You can't spend all your
time daydreaming."

"You want to catch up to me someday,
don't you, champ?" Mr. Murphy added from
behind his paper. Noah frowned. He *did*
want to grow as big as his father, but not
today. Today he had other dreams. Rather
than growing taller, Noah Murphy was
dreaming of shrinking, shrinking to the size
of his little guys.

Noah looked down at the Commander,
who was leaning rigidly against his cereal
bowl. The Commander's eyes, two little dots
of blue, remained unchanged. Noah sat re-
membering how they'd looked when the

Commander had come alive before. They'd been a deep blue and his skin had crinkled around them when he smiled. Noah looked into his bowl at Gordy, and spooned some oatmeal over his foot. He thought about Gordy, too. When he was alive, he'd had a really goofy giggle. No one was giggling now, though. The Commander and Gordy were motionless, trapped in the cold silence of hard plastic.

"Noah Murphy, what are you dreaming about, staring off into space like that?" Mrs. Murphy demanded.

"My guys," Noah mumbled. "Just my guys."

Again he looked at the Commander and Gordy. You know what I'm dreaming about, don't you, guys? Noah thought. I'm dreaming of the day I'll find the magic powder, and we'll have another adventure. That's what I'm dreaming about. The day you'll come alive and we'll be together again, back in action.

CHAPTER TWO

"Hey!" Jess blurted out, seeing the top of Gordy's head sticking out of Noah's oatmeal. Mrs. Murphy was picking up some banana slices from the floor, and Mr. Murphy was still lost in his newspaper. Noah quickly shot Jess a look. He didn't want his little brother to draw the grown-ups' attention to Gordy. Jess winked and Jack sat watching intently from his high chair.

Now that Noah had an audience, he suddenly felt brave. He waited for Mrs. Murphy to go to the sink with some dishes and then he quickly reached into his oatmeal and made Gordy sit up. Jess beamed with delight, and Jack hooted with laughter.

Gordy's head was covered with pieces of soggy cereal. He looked ridiculous. Noah turned Gordy upside down, making him do a headstand in the oatmeal.

"Good old Gordy," Jess whispered.

Noah dropped Gordy again, then turned to Jess.

"Someday I'm going to find that magic powder," Noah whispered. "And as soon as I do, Gordy and the Commander will be back in action."

"Back in action?" Mr. Murphy looked up from his paper.

"Uh . . . yeah, Dad," Noah stammered, spooning oatmeal over Gordy again. "That's what I always say . . . uh . . . before I have my guys go on another adventure."

"What an imagination," Mr. Murphy muttered, looking back at his paper. Noah knew that he had an imagination, but he also knew that the adventure he was thinking of had nothing to do with his imagination. This new adventure was going to be real. Gordy and the Commander were going to become real and Noah was really going to shrink down to their size.

Noah knew this could happen because it had happened once before. It all began last year, when he bought a tiny magic kit at a gum and toy machine in the supermarket. Noah had taken the "magic powder" out of the kit's bag and sprinkled it on himself and his guys. Then he had made a wish that the Commander and Gordy would come alive and that he would shrink down to have an adventure with them.

To his amazement, Noah found that the magic powder had actually worked. The Commander and Gordy had come alive, and Noah had suddenly shrunk down to just four inches tall. They had spent all day at school, narrowly escaping the jaws of the fourth grade's pet hamster and almost getting stomped to death in the school cafeteria. It was an adventure that Noah would never forget.

Once everything had returned to normal, Noah had discovered that there was still some magic powder left in the bag. Noah promised his best friend, Nate Cooper, that he could come on the next adventure.

The two boys had met in Noah's bedroom the following Saturday to use the magic powder. But when they'd got there, they'd discovered it was missing. They had turned the bedroom upside down, looking for the little plastic bag, but they'd never found it. After that, Noah's daydreams were filled with the adventures that he and his guys could go on together, if only he could find the powder.

From then on Nate had been coming over every Saturday morning to help Noah look for it. At first, the two boys spent hours tearing apart Noah's room. As the months passed, however, they spent less time looking, until finally they were searching for only a few minutes.

This Saturday morning, as Noah waited for Nate to arrive, he heard Overdue bark. Overdue was the Murphys' dog. As a puppy, he had eaten so many overdue library books that the Murphys had decided to call him Overdue Books, or Overdue for short. As he got older, Overdue outgrew his love for library books, overdue or otherwise. This was a relief to Mrs. Murphy, since she was a librarian and found it embarrassing that a member of her family digested so many books. Noah and Jess were equally relieved, since they were held responsible for their dog's destructive eating habits and had to pay for the half-eaten books out of their allowances.

Overdue was barking now, as the doorbell rang.

"I'll get it," Noah cried, jumping out of his seat. "It's probably Nate." But before he could leave the table, Mrs. Murphy stopped him cold.

"Hold it right there," she said briskly. "Your father will answer the door. You can finish up your breakfast and then I want you and Jess to look after Jack for me while I take a shower."

"Oh, but Mom," Noah objected, "Nate came over to play, not to baby-sit."

"Jack can play with you," Mrs. Murphy suggested. "Just be sure to shut your bedroom door so he doesn't run out into the hall."

"He can't play with us. He's only two years old!"

"He's your cousin," Mrs. Murphy reminded him.

"He's Destructo Man in diapers, that's who he is," Noah wailed. "Whenever we let him come in our room, he wrecks everything in sight!"

"I'll only be in the shower for a few minutes," Mrs. Murphy assured him.

"Oh, but Mom . . ." Noah was suddenly interrupted by the sound of a loud crash that came from the living room.

"Good grief! Not this string thing again!" Mr. Murphy bellowed. Noah looked over at Jess who was sinking down into his seat.

"Jess Murphy, didn't I tell you that there were to be no more of your string traps in this house?" shouted his father.

Mrs. Murphy shook her head as she peeked into the living room.

"It was only a small one," Jess said in a little voice. He had slumped so far down in

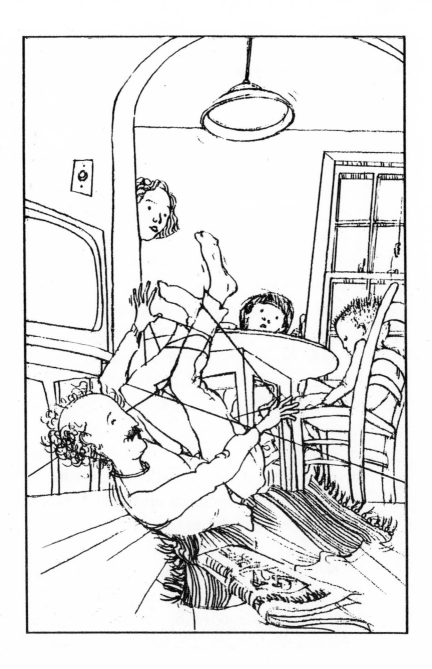

his chair only the reddish-brown bristles of his flattopped haircut could be seen.

Noah grinned. He knew that Jess was fascinated by how things work. He was always taking apart his toys and putting them back together again. Lately, he had started making string traps. He would wind string around the furniture in complicated patterns, then wait for people to get caught and work their way out.

"One more string trap and your allowance is canceled for life," Mr. Murphy yelled.

Noah heard the door open and Nate's high-pitched laugh. Nate was the smallest boy in the fifth grade and his voice was the highest.

"Hi, Mr. Murphy, what's with all the string?" Nate asked. "Were you trying to fly a kite or something? I once had a cousin who got all caught up in kite string and he . . ."

"No, Nate, I was not trying to fly a kite," Mr. Murphy said through clenched teeth, pulling some string off his leg.

Nate walked into the kitchen and stood

beside Noah. Mr. Murphy followed him, turning his attention to Jess.

"This string business has got to stop," Mr. Murphy said gravely, beginning a lengthy lecture. Mrs. Murphy was scouring some pots.

It was the right moment for a daring rescue. Noah reached into his oatmeal bowl and lifted out Gordy. He stuffed him into his sweatshirt pocket, along with the Commander. Then he hurriedly shoveled a few spoonfuls of oatmeal into his mouth.

"We're out of here," Noah whispered to Nate, standing up.

"Don't forget Jack," Mrs. Murphy called to him from the sink.

"Can't Dad watch him?" Noah pleaded.

"No, your father is going to be busy cleaning the cellar," Mrs. Murphy replied.

"I am?" Mr. Murphy asked, a stricken look coming over his face.

"Now, you know you are, Mark," Mrs. Murphy huffed. "You promised that you'd have it cleaned up this weekend. Oh, but before you start, dear, would you take Jack out of his high chair, so the boys can take him upstairs with them?"

Noah's shoulders slumped as he watched his father take Jack down from the chair.

Jack came toddling over to Noah, dragging his ugly AckAck by the neck. He stretched his arm up to his big cousin, and Noah reluctantly took his little hand. Jack cooed happily, pressing a piece of banana into Noah's palm.

"Oh, yuck!" Noah moaned, wiping the banana on his pants.

"AckAck, AckAck," Jack sang, holding his toy up for Nate to see.

"Just what I feel like doing on a Saturday morning," Noah muttered. "Baby-sitting for Destructo Man and his monster!"

CHAPTER THREE

"So what do you want to do after the search?" Nate asked, closing the bedroom door.

Noah was sitting on his bed next to Jack and AckAck. Jess had given Jack a hairbrush and the toddler was busy brushing AckAck's nonexistent hair.

"Well, we can work on the space station," Noah suggested. The space station was the Murphy brothers' latest building project. They were always working on something in their room, either castles or forts or space stations. They had started this new station a few days ago. It was a unique structure, standing about two feet high, constructed of wooden and plastic blocks, cardboard, and sticks. It was positioned at the foot of Noah's bed.

"But we'll have to take turns keeping an eye on Jack," Noah said. "Jess, why don't you watch him first, then Nate can take a turn."

"And when do you get to watch him?" Jess asked.

"I can't watch him if I have to supervise the construction of the space station, Jess," Noah explained.

"And just why do you always get to be the one to supervise?" Jess wanted to know.

"Because the station was my idea," Noah told him, taking Gordy and the Commander out of his pocket and laying them on his bed. "And for another thing, we're using most of my blocks to build it."

Jess shrugged and walked over to the bed. "OK, OK," muttered Jess, sitting down beside his little cousin. "But Nate's the big baby lover. Why doesn't he watch Jack?"

It was true, Nate did love babies and puppies and kittens.

"I need Nate to design the runways and launchpads. He can take over with Jack when he finishes that," Noah said, sliding off the bed.

Jack giggled and picked up Gordy. Before Jess or Noah could stop him, the toddler had put the little plastic figure in his mouth. He began to lick off all of Gordy's oatmeal.

"Well, I guess the little guy comes in handy for something." Nate laughed.

"Gordy hates taking a bath," Noah said, pulling Gordy away from Jack. "I wonder how he feels about being licked clean. Just think of the stories that he could tell us, like what it was like to be inside of Destructo Man's mouth." Noah walked over to the closet and began looking through the baskets of toys. "Once we find the magic powder, Gordy can tell us all kinds of things."

"Noah, when are you going to give up?" Jess said, shaking his head. "You've looked for that magic powder for a whole year and the chances of you finding it now are almost impossible."

"Why?" Noah wanted to know. "Why is it impossible?"

"Because so much time has passed since

you last saw it," Jess told him. "All kinds of things could have happened to the powder by now. It could have been thrown out with the garbage, or sucked up by Mom's vacuum cleaner or eaten by Overdue. What do you say, Nate? Don't you think I'm right?"

Nate stole a guilty look at Jess, not wanting to side against his friend. "It has been a whole year," he said gently.

Noah shrugged. "Fine, don't help me look, then. But I'll tell you this," he added, searching through a box of puzzle pieces, "I'm never going to stop looking, because I remember what the Commander and Gordy were like when they were alive and I know it can happen again. It just has to, and when it does, I'm going to have the most incredible adventure of my life." His voice broke into a sob and he quickly turned so that no one would see the tears filling his eyes.

"I guess it won't hurt to look a little longer," Nate said, glancing at Jess. He picked up a toy basket and emptied it out on the rug. "Hey, Noah," Nate called, "come over and look at this stuff. We haven't gone through this basket in a long time." Noah sat down beside his friend, and the two began sorting through the toys, searching for the tiny bag of powder.

"These little plastic computers would be great for the screening room of the station," Nate said, holding up the tiny blue and yellow plastic blocks that were painted to look like computers.

"And how about these catapults from my castle set?" Noah added. "We can position them on the outer walkways. That way we'd have a defense system in case of alien invasion." Before long, the boys had forgotten all about searching for the magic powder and were hard at work fortifying the space station.

"Why don't we use those rocks that we brought up from the creek? We can make a wall," Nate suggested.

"Cool idea, Nate." Noah got up and walked over to the rocks that were piled next to the closet. The two boys quickly built a rock wall around the entire space station. "This wall will be our first barrier,"

Noah decided, climbing over it. "But we'll need some kind of ammunition for the catapults," he said, fixing the last plastic catapult in place on the roof of the station.

"Jess, how about your marbles?" Noah suggested. "They would be perfect." He looked over at the bed, just in time to see AckAck go flying through the air and land on the rug. Jack was bouncing on Jess's stomach. He stopped for a minute and hurled Noah's hairbrush after his hairless monster. It narrowly missed Nate's eye, and crashed into one of the monitoring towers.

"Thanks for thinking of me, Jack, but I've already brushed my hair today," said Nate.

"Looks like you're going to need more than marbles to defend yourself." Jess grinned.

"I don't think the alien invasion will be as devastating as Jack's attack," Noah replied. "The marbles will be perfect ammunition."

"I have to get them out of my backpack," said Jess, jumping off the bed. "Nate, it's your turn to baby-sit the beast."

Nate climbed on the bed beside Jack and

the toddler giggled and kissed him on the nose. Jess, meanwhile, got the marbles and placed them on the roof of the station.

"I'll get more catapults," Noah said, going to the closet. "Hey, here's an old box full of art supplies. I forgot we even had it. And look, we almost forgot the Zoomlor." He reached down and picked up a toy spaceship.

"What's a Zoomlor?" Nate wanted to know.

"That's our latest vehicle," Jess told him. Besides stations and forts, Noah and Jess spent a lot of time building vehicles. They made them out of interlocking plastic blocks. They were just big enough to hold a few of Noah's guys. At first Noah and Jess had built simple planes and rockets, but as the brothers became more experienced and accumulated more blocks, they put together ships that were sophisticated and complex. This latest ship was their best yet. Jess had designed an instrument panel complete with computers, flashing lights, and high-tech landing gear. The ship was a masterpiece.

"This reminds me of the Doomsdipper on Air Patrol," Nate exclaimed, as he examined the purple-and-silver spaceship. "Boy, I love that machine." Jack was now bouncing on his stomach.

"How did you do at the Video Arcade yesterday?" Jess asked. Nate was reigning champion of Air Patrol, a video flight game.

"How I always do." Nate beamed. "When it comes to flight, I'm a natural. Nobody can beat me. I've flown so many missions for Air Patrol, I could probably get on a real plane and fly it blindfolded.

"I've got all the model airplanes that Hobby Hangout sells, except for the SX510," Nate continued. "But as soon as I save up for it, I'll buy that one, too. If you need to know anything about flying, just ask me. Why I can . . . I can . . ." Nate suddenly grew quiet and a funny look came over his face. Noah and Jess looked up from the rug and even Jack sat staring.

"You can what?" Jess asked.

"I can tell you anything about flying," Nate said, wrinkling his nose, "but when it comes to diapers, I don't think I'm the man for the job."

"Don't worry," Noah laughed. "My mom is on Diaper Patrol this weekend." He went to the door and called Mrs. Murphy. She came running into the bedroom with her hair wrapped in a towel.

"It's about time we got you out of these pajamas," she said, picking Jack up. She gave her nephew a kiss and walked to the door. "Come on, little Jack," she cooed, carrying him into the bathroom.

"Little Jack the Maniac forgot his trusty monster AckAck," Nate said, noticing the plastic monster lying on the rug.

"We'll give it to him when we're through working," Noah decided. He looked over at Jess, who was busy taping his "instrument panels" to the station's walls. He had used his best colored markers to draw tiny computers and mapping screens onto a piece of construction paper. He looked up at Noah and grinned. "What do you think?"

"Great!" Noah nodded. "Now all we need are some victory supplies."

"Victory supplies?" Jess looked puzzled. Noah went to the closet. He pulled out the old cardboard box full of art supplies. He placed several tubes of glitter on the station's roof, next to the marble supply.

"We can use glitter to celebrate our victories," Noah explained, taking the top off a plastic tube. He quickly poured a small amount of gold glitter into one of the station's catapults. When he released the firing mechanism, a golden shower exploded in the air.

"Wow," Jess whispered, as the glittering sprinkles rained down on the rug. "Mom is going to kill us if she finds out we're celebrating our victories like this!"

"Oh, she won't find out, Jess," Noah assured him. "We haven't used the stuff in this box for so long, she probably doesn't remember that we still have it. We'll just have to clean it up when we're done."

"How much glitter are you going to use?" Nate asked, brushing his finger over the sparkling rug.

"All of it," Noah said. "We'll have a major

battle with an alien planet and then when we win, we'll have a major celebration!" He rummaged around in the art box, looking for all the tubes of glitter he could find. "It'll be neat to use a lot of different colors. I know we had some green glitter in here somewhere." Suddenly Noah's eyes grew wide and his mouth dropped open.

"What?" Jess wanted to know. "What's the matter?"

"I found it!" Noah croaked.

"Found what?" Nate asked. "The green glitter?"

"Look, I found it!" Noah whispered, his hand trembling as he held up a tiny bag of silver powder.

"That glitter isn't green, it's silver." Nate was confused. He turned to Jess, whose eyes had become as large as Noah's.

"No, it's not silver glitter," Jess mumbled. "It's not glitter at all. It's . . . it's the magic powder, Nate. He really did it! Noah found the magic powder!"

CHAPTER FOUR

"You mean you really found it?" Nate gasped. "That's the magic powder?"

Noah held the little clear bag of silver powder up to his face.

"That's it, all right," he whispered.

"I can't believe this," Jess said, unable to take his eyes off the little bag.

"Mom must have found the magic powder when she was cleaning our room. She probably thought it was silver glitter and threw it in the old art box," Noah said excitedly. He crawled underneath his bed.

"What are you doing now?" Nate asked.

"Trying to decide which of my guys to take along," Noah told him. He pulled out the shoe boxes that were filled with his action figures.

"You're not *really* going to use the powder again, are you?" Jess croaked.

"Are you kidding? Of course I am!" Noah exclaimed. "It's the experience of a lifetime. Come on, don't be so wimpy. It doesn't hurt, I promise."

"I'm not wimpy," Jess sniffed. "Just careful. Shrinking down to four inches may not hurt, but what happens when someone who is five feet tall steps on you? Are you going to tell me that won't hurt?"

"Jess, you'll never have fun if all you do is worry about the bad things that can happen." Noah sighed. "You won't even blow a bubble with your bubble gum because you're afraid you'll get gum on your face when the bubble breaks. You're missing out on some of the best things in life. Right, Nate?"

"Oh, yeah, I blow bubbles all the time," Nate stammered. "I've got this cousin who blew this bubble once . . ."

"Not now, Nate," Noah interrupted.

"We've got to make our plans for the adventure."

"The adventure, right," Nate said weakly. "Tell me again how it works."

"We sprinkle the magic powder on us, and then on the Commander and Gordy. I make a wish for them to come alive, and for us to be able to shrink down so we can have an adventure with them," Noah explained. "How about Gargantuan Man? Should we take him along?" He held up a little plastic green man full of muscles.

Nate frowned. "Do you really think it's a good idea to go today?" he whispered.

"Of course we have to go today!" Noah exclaimed. "We've been waiting for a whole year to go on this adventure." He put Gargantuan Man back in the shoe box. "I think it should just be you and me and the Commander and Gordy, since the last time the aliens had so much trouble."

"Don't you remember how dangerous it was the last time?" Jess asked.

"Dangerous?" Noah shook his head. "Jess, it's dangerous to breathe today! Our air is polluted, our food is full of cancer germs, candy is bad for us and TV can give us radiation. If we stopped to worry about everything we do, we'd never do anything. You can't be a wimp all your life."

Jess frowned and lowered his eyes. "I'm not a wimp," he said. "Who went on the Scream Machine roller coaster at Dorney Park last year?"

"You only went on that because your friend, Mark Freer, paid you three dollars to do it. Then you threw up all over the money when you got off. I wouldn't call that too courageous." Noah smirked, but when he looked at his little brother's troubled face, he knew that Jess couldn't help being so careful. It was just the way he was.

"I guess it's better that you're not coming with us," Noah decided. "We could really use someone your size to look after us, the way you did the last time."

"Well, OK." Jess hesitated. "But what if you can't get back to your normal size?"

"Don't worry, Jess. The Commander explained it when he came to life," Noah told him. "Once the adventure is over, everything returns to normal. There's nothing to worry about."

"Nothing?" Jess asked, his forehead wrinkling with worry.

"OK, everything," Noah said. "There is everything to worry about, but everything to look forward to, too." He turned to face Nate. "Any adventure worth having is dangerous. You're not afraid, are you, Nate?"

"Who me? No, I'm not afraid, not really," Nate said, his voice trailing off. Actually he looked terrified, now that they were really about to do it. "Aren't you afraid? Even a little?" he asked.

"Sure, a little," Noah admitted. "It's always scary to try new things, but they can turn out to be great things."

"Yeah, I know," Nate said, trying to smile. "It's just that I wasn't planning on doing anything great today."

Noah could tell that Nate was nervous. He was biting the inside of his lower lip, and his voice had risen about two octaves.

"If you're afraid to come with me, Nate, just say so," Noah said impatiently.

"Who said that I was afraid?" cried Nate. "I want to go, really I do." Nate sounded as convincing as he could.

"I knew I could depend on you, Nate," said Noah.

Nate smiled limply and sat down on the bed. Noah reached for the little plastic figure that was on his pillow. "Well, Commander, it won't be long now," he whispered in his ear.

"It sure will be weird being that small." Nate gulped, looking over at the Commander, who was sitting in the palm of Noah's hand.

"Weird and wonderful," Noah said, opening the bag of magic powder. "This is it, Nate. Are you with me?"

"I'm with you," Nate said, giving the thumbs-up sign.

"Great," Noah whispered, giving the thumbs-up back. He turned to his brother. "We really can count on you to look out for us, right, Jess?"

Jess tried to smile but he couldn't, since

he was too worried. "I wish you weren't doing this," he said. "But OK, I'll try and keep
an eye on you."

"That ought to be a pretty big eye once
we're their size." Noah winked as he placed
the Commander back on the pillow beside
Gordy.

"This is the scariest thing I've ever done,"
Nate said, leaning back on the bed, next to
Noah.

"Aw, come on, Nate. Just last week you
were telling me about the meatless meat loaf
your sister Allison made for supper. That
had to be pretty scary. This adventure will
be a lot less painful. It'll be fun, you'll see,"
Noah told him, taking a bit of the powder
from the bag and sprinkling it on the Commander and then on Gordy. There wasn't
much left, so he carefully dipped his finger
into the rest and brushed a little on the back
of Nate's hand, then on his own. Noah
handed the bag to Jess. "Put it somewhere
safe," he told him. "There's still a tiny bit
left." Then he gazed over at the two little
figures on the pillow.

"Let them come to life," Noah whispered, "and let Nate and me shrink to their size, so we can all go on an adventure to . . ." But before Noah could finish, Nate sneezed so hard that bits of the magic powder from his hand blew into the air. Noah watched, wide-eyed, as the silvery particles rained down on the shoe boxes at Nate's feet.

Suddenly everything went black. The room began to spin. Noah closed his eyes. He felt as if he were turning round and round. There was a loud buzzing sound in his ears. After a few seconds everything began to slow down. He opened his eyes and saw a wall of green before him. Jess had suddenly become a mountain of green sweatshirt. But it wasn't Jess who had changed. Noah was the one who had changed. He was only four and a half inches tall! Nate stood beside him, just under four inches.

"It worked! It worked!" Noah squeaked, looking over at his miniature friend. "Isn't this great, Nate? Are you OK?"

"I'm . . . I'm OK," Nate managed to

mumble. "Everything is so big! It's just that I've always dreamed about being taller, not shorter. It's like being in another world!" The two little figures were standing ankle deep in the blue fuzz of the blanket.

"It *is* like another world, but don't worry, Nate, we've got Jess here to help us out, right, Jess?" Noah looked up at his giant little brother. Jess was about to speak when someone knocked on the bedroom door. Noah and Nate quickly put their hands over their ears, but they were still able to hear Jess's thunderous cry.

"Dad!" Jess exclaimed as Mr. Murphy walked into the bedroom.

CHAPTER FIVE

"Dad! Oh, hi, Dad. I wasn't sure who it was," Jess stammered.

"Yes, it's me," said Mr. Murphy. "And I would hazard a guess that you're someone they call Jess." He came up beside his youngest son. "I can tell that you must be a son of mine just by looking at your feet." Mr. Murphy pointed down at Jess's socks. Jess's socks never matched. Today he had a blue one on his left foot and a gray one on his right foot. Mr. Murphy was wearing two different-colored socks, too.

"Yes, you're definitely a son of mine," Mr. Murphy laughed. "Well, now that we all know who we are, I am here to deliver a message from your mother. She said that you're to report to the den on the double. It seems that Mrs. Plumbio is coming over this morning to give you a piano lesson. Your mother almost forgot about it."

"But I've already had my lesson this week," Jess protested.

"I know," Mr. Murphy said, "but your mother made arrangements with Mrs. P. to give you a makeup lesson for the one you missed last week. Hurry down now, Mrs. Plumbio will be here any minute. And where is what's-his-name and that friend of his?"

"Wha . . . what's his name?" Jess croaked, standing so that his back was to the little figures that were sitting on the blanket. But it was too late. His father was looking directly at Noah and Nate.

"You know, that kid who's always leaving behind a trail of those little guys," Mr. Murphy said, pointing to what he thought were two toys. "What's his name?" he teased.

Jess was stunned. His father was looking at Noah and Nate and not even recognizing them. Since Mr. Murphy was a grown-up, he was unable to see the magic that was right before his eyes. He had no idea that one of the little toy figures on the bed was actually his firstborn son.

"Noah? Oh, he's with Nate," Jess said truthfully.

"I know he's with Nate," Mr. Murphy said, "but I thought they came up here to play."

"Uh . . . they did come up here," Jess stammered. "But then they went off on this big adventure."

Mr. Murphy laughed and shook his head. "A big adventure, hey? Well, if they show up, you tell your brother that there is a big adventure waiting for him in the cellar. I want you two to clean up the mess you made down there last week." Mr. Murphy walked to the door and turned to look back at Jess. "Your mother tells me that your little cousin went through this house like a cyclone yesterday."

"Jack's a crazy little kid, all right," Jess said.

"We'll have our hands full looking after

him today. I just wish Noah had mentioned that he was going off to play so early," Mr. Murphy muttered. "Well, it looks like it's just the two of us, Jess. As soon as your lesson is over, you can report for duty in the cellar."

Jess's shoulders slumped. "I've got some important stuff I planned on doing today, Dad," he told him.

"I'm sure it can wait until after the cellar is done," Mr. Murphy said.

"But, Dad, Noah is getting to do what he wants, can't I work on the cellar after I do what I want?" Jess pleaded.

"Oh, all right," Mr. Murphy said with a sigh. "I suppose it wouldn't hurt to do it later, as long as it gets done sometime today." As soon as Mr. Murphy had left the room, Jess ran over to close the door. But just then his mother came rushing in from the bathroom. She had Jack in her arms.

"Jess," she cried, "did Dad tell you about your piano lesson? Mrs. Plumbio will be here any second! You know how she hates to be kept waiting. Let me see how you look. Did you brush your teeth? Oh, look at your socks!" She groaned. "Put your sneakers on, honey, and Mrs. Plumbio will never know how mismatched you are. And, Jess, try to concentrate on your lesson today. Mrs. Plumbio feels that you aren't giving your lessons your full attention."

"But, Mom, I've got some other stuff that I have . . ."

"No buts," Mrs. Murphy said firmly. "You missed one lesson last week. Hurry downstairs. You can practice a bit before Mrs. Plumbio gets here."

"But, Mom . . ." Jess moaned.

"I said no buts." Mrs. Murphy frowned, pointing to the stairs. Unlike her husband, Mrs. Murphy was always direct and forceful. There was nothing scatterbrained about her, and while Mr. Murphy could usually be talked into things, Mrs. Murphy stood firm, a pillar of strength and determination, with her socks always matching.

"Could I just check on something in my room?" Jess pleaded.

"There's no time, Jess. Your room isn't going anywhere. It will be here when you get back, I promise," she said, waiting for him to move.

"My room may be here when I get back, but where will Noah and Nate be?" Jess muttered. He trudged past his mother and made his way reluctantly down the stairs.

Meanwhile, the four little figures on the bed were beginning to move. Gordy and the Commander were on the pillow and Noah and Nate were on the blanket below.

"What are we going to do without Jess to help us?" Nate cried. Noah gulped, trying to swallow away the sudden panic that was overtaking him.

"Don't worry, Nate, Jess will only be downstairs in the study for half an hour. He'll be back." Noah tried to reassure his friend, as well as himself. "We've got to find the Commander and Gordy—they'll know what to do."

"This feels so weird," Nate squeaked, turning his head to look at the miles of blue fuzz stretching out before him.

"Let's try over there," Noah said, pointing to what looked like a giant white wall.

"What is it?" Nate asked.

"I think it's my pillow, at least I hope it is," Noah said, tilting his head to scan the top of the pillow. "Gordy and the Commander should be up there somewhere. Commander, can you hear me?" Noah yelled. But there was no reply. "Hey, Commander, are you up there?"

Nate was crawling along the edge of the pillow to its opening. "Wow! What smells so good?" he cried, walking into the pillowcase.

"Nate, where are you?" Noah called.

"Here I am!" Nate yelled, sticking his head out of the pillowcase. "It smells like heaven in here," he said, as Noah stepped into the case beside him. "If my pillow smelled like this, I would never want to get out of bed."

"Oh, gee!" Noah exclaimed. "I forgot. I

stashed some candy in there. It was left over from the movies last week."

"This is paradise," Nate squeaked. "If we're this small, just think how big that candy will be."

"Um . . . You're right," Noah agreed. "But we shouldn't go looking for candy until we hook up with the Commander and Gordy."

"Oh, come on, let's just have a taste, I mean a look," Nate said, walking farther into the case. Noah followed. They hadn't gotten far when they came upon a pile of long red logs, with some giant pieces of bubble gum beside them.

"Gosh!" Nate exclaimed, running up to the huge sticks of licorice. "They're as big as trees! And look at the bubble gum. This piece is so heavy that I can't lift it!" he cried. He took his penknife out of his back pocket and began cutting through the gum's wrapper.

Noah was walking farther into the pillowcase, stumbling upon a giant roll of Lifesavers. He had eaten half the roll at the movies last Saturday, and had saved the rest. After struggling to pull down the wrapper, he stood back with a grin. He was looking at the biggest red Lifesaver that he had ever seen in his life.

CHAPTER SIX

"Hey, Nate, wait till you see what I've found," Noah called. He reached up and pried a huge Lifesaver loose. Noah was about to roll it over to his friend, when he decided to have a few licks first. "Nate," he yelled again, "you're going to love this."

"A bit early in the day to be hitting the hard stuff, wouldn't you say?" a familiar voice replied.

Noah looked up to see the Commander standing before him, tall and with wide shoulders. He didn't look like a grown-up, all serious and boring, but he didn't look goofy or scatterbrained either. No, the Commander looked like a hero, daring like a boy and experienced like a man. His chin was firm, yet his eyes lit up and matched a smile that let you know he liked to take a chance, liked the thrill of facing danger.

"Commander!" Noah shouted. "You're back! You're alive! You look great!"

"You look pretty good yourself." The Commander laughed, reaching out to give Noah a hug. For a second, Noah trembled, realizing that only minutes earlier he had been holding this man in the palm of his hand.

"Looks like an interesting adventure ahead of us," the Commander said, tweaking his brown mustache.

"But what about Gordy?" Noah asked. "Isn't he with you?"

"I'm afraid my faithful comrade has fallen under the influence of some pretty powerful bubble gum." The Commander shook his head in mock horror. "When we entered the pillowcase, Gordy saw Nate carving up all that gum, and he decided that Nate was in urgent need of assistance. I couldn't drag

him away, although we'd better give it another try now, before he and Nate chew
themselves into unconsciousness." He
turned and Noah followed him back through
the pillowcase. When they had almost
reached the opening, they saw Nate and
Gordy lying on their backs. Their faces were
completely covered by the huge bubbles
they were blowing.

"Good grief, Gordy!" the Commander
cried. "How many times do I have to tell
you not to blow such big bubbles? You've
got gum all over yourself." The Commander
sighed. "I'll have to give you another haircut."

"Why?" Nate asked, after taking a giant
wad of gum out of his mouth.

"Just look at him." The Commander
frowned. "How else can we get that gum out
of his hair?"

There was gum all over Gordy's face and in
his hair. "Gee, Commander, isn't a fella en-
titled to a little fun? After all, I've been
through a traumatic experience this morn-

ing, and I'm still not over the trauma of it all."

"You mean the trauma of coming to life?" Noah asked.

"No," Gordy muttered, pulling some gum from his nose. "I mean the trauma of having to do a headstand in a bowl of oatmeal. I'm going to have nightmares about that mission for a long time. It's a good thing you've got all this gum here. It helps me to forget for a little while." He shook his head. "You should have seen that last bubble, Noah, it was a beauty."

"That's enough bragging about your bubble gum exploits." The Commander took out his field scissors. "Now, sit still, Gordy, while I cut this stuff out." The Commander proceeded to give Gordy a haircut, while Nate carved up the rest of the gum with his penknife.

"We'll have a lifetime's supply!" Nate cried.

"Only if you spend your life being four inches tall," Noah reminded him.

"Oh, rats, I forgot about that," Nate said, putting his knife away.

"Hey, Nate, don't forget your friends over

here," Gordy called out. "You can cut up a few more pieces for me. I'm not planning on getting any taller."

"And I'm not planning on giving you another haircut," the Commander told him. "You've had enough gum today, Gordy."

"Well, OK, but let's not forget about tomorrow," Gordy said, cocking his head, so that the Commander almost cut off his ear. "Don't forget your favorite saying, Commander: 'A man on a mission has to think two steps ahead of the game if he wants to win.' Go ahead, Nate, cut me up some more chunks. I've got plenty of room. I can stuff them in my pack."

"Why is it, Gordy, that the only time you choose to remember a sound piece of military strategy is when you're thinking of bubble gum?" The Commander shook his head.

As Nate filled Gordy's pack with the large blocks of gum, some muffled sounds were coming from the floor.

"What's that?" Noah asked.

"I don't know," Nate whispered. They all grew quiet as the rumbling grew louder.

"We had better check it out," the Commander said. Noah, Nate, and Gordy stood up and followed him out of the pillowcase and across the bed. When they reached the edge, the Commander ordered everyone to lie on their stomachs. "We're less likely to be targets this way," he told them.

"Targets for who?" Nate whispered to Noah, his voice shaky with fear.

"I don't know, Nate," Noah whispered back. "Just listen to the Commander. He knows what he's doing." Noah tried to sound as confident as he could, but he was suddenly feeling small, very small, and that didn't make him feel confident at all.

"Oh, no," Noah cried, looking down at the rug, "I don't believe it!"

"Believe what?" Nate squeaked.

"Look down there," Noah gasped in horror, pointing to a shoe box near the bed.

"My guys!" Noah whispered. "Look, they're alive! They're all alive!"

CHAPTER SEVEN

Everyone looked down at the open shoe box. It was filled with a squirming mass of pink bodies struggling to get free.

"You must have blown some of the magic powder on them when you sneezed, Nate!" Noah cried.

"Those are your little wrestlers, aren't they, Noah?" the Commander asked.

"Yes," Noah gasped. "I began collecting them last year. They're the smallest guys in my collection. There must be hundreds of them in that box, and they're all alive!"

"Look," Nate whispered, "a few of them are trying to stand."

"Those little wrestlers are half-pints," said

Gordy. "They only come up to my knee!"

"They may be half-pints," Noah whispered, "but they're incredibly strong half-pints. Do you see the one in the middle? That's Crunch." Everyone looked down to see a short pink wrestler giving orders to his comrades. Crunch was the shortest but the strongest, since he had the most muscles. He even looked as if he had muscles in his earlobes.

"Let's get moving, don't stand and gape," Crunch commanded. "If we're going to break out of here, we've got to get in shape."

When Noah had played with Crunch, he'd always made him talk in rhyme.

"That Crunch is a born leader," the Commander whispered. "I'm impressed."

"I always knew Crunch had what it takes." Noah watched Crunch direct his strongest men to line up along one wall of the box. It wasn't long before Crunch was directing a second group to climb up on the shoulders of the first group. Soon the entire side of the shoe box was lined with the little wrestlers. They stood balancing on each other's shoulders, huffing and puffing, as they helped one another up.

"All right, line three, climb up, flip-flup," Crunch ordered the next group.

"Flip-flup? Who's he trying to kid?" Gordy smirked.

"Shh, Gordy, quiet," the Commander ordered. "The little fellow is doing the best he can."

Even though Crunch's rhyming was not the best, he did seem to have control of the situation. Dutifully the sweaty little wrestlers raced up their brothers' backs and onto their shoulders. As the last line scaled the mountain of little pink men, the shoe box began to tilt.

"Heave, heave," shouted Crunch, as he desperately tried to think of something to rhyme with heave.

"Heave, heave, up your uncle's sleeve!" he finally yelled. Together the wrestlers pushed on the box until it fell over with a loud crash. There was quite an uproar as the men tumbled out onto the rug. Once free, the wrestlers began shoving and pushing each other around. Crunch tried to calm them down, but they started shouting above his calls for order.

"What's happening?" Noah yelled. The crowd of wrestlers had become so loud that Noah had to yell to be heard. "Why aren't they listening to Crunch anymore?"

"I'm not sure," the Commander said, surveying the scene below. "It could be because they're out of their box. The wrestlers look to Crunch as their commander as long as they're in the shoe box, but now that they're free, he doesn't seem to have any control." The Commander quickly got to his feet. "If we don't do something now," he said, turning to Noah, "Crunch may be in grave danger. The wrestlers are getting ugly. They need to see their real leader."

"Who's that?" Noah stammered.

"Who do you think?" the Commander said, helping Noah to his feet. Noah stood dazed. He watched as the Commander called down to the crowd, "Stop!" Suddenly hundreds of little pink eyes were looking upward. The Commander stood bravely hold-

ing out his arms. "There will be no fighting,"
he ordered in a firm, steady voice. No one
moved or spoke, until Slam, the largest
wrestler, threw back his head.

"Says who?" he yelled up to the Commander.

"Says Noah," the Commander shouted
down, motioning for Noah to come closer to
the edge of the bed. On hearing this and
seeing the miniature Noah, all the wrestlers
seemed to gasp in unison.

"Noah! Noah! Noah! . . ." The room was
filled with the chant as they reverently whispered his name. Noah gulped and waved a
shaky hand down to them.

CHAPTER EIGHT

"Commander, do they all know me?" Noah croaked, looking at the hundreds of little pink faces.

"Of course. You've been playing with them since last year, haven't you?"

"Well, yes, but this is different. Now that they're alive, I can't . . ."

"Oh, yes, you can. You're their leader. They look up to you."

"Way up," Gordy grinned, leaning over the edge of the bed as he waved to the wrestlers below. "Hey, Commander, if Noah is their leader, doesn't that make us kind of next in command?"

"Not now, Gordy. We've got a crisis situation on our hands," said the Commander. He turned to Noah. "You've got to talk to them and reassure them that you're still in charge. It would be chaos if they were left on their own."

"Hey, look at Crunch," Nate interrupted. "It looks like he's trying to get our attention." Crunch was waving his arms over his head. When the little wrestler saw that Noah was looking at him, he put his arms down and called up in his loudest voice.

"Hello, Noah, sir, glad to see your fur. Er, sorry, sir. Let me start again. You're not very tall. I wonder how you got so small, not that it matters at all." Crunch blushed a deep rose color, since he had never done so much rhyming in front of such a large audience.

The Commander gave Noah a nudge and whispered in his ear, "Go ahead, Noah. They're waiting for you."

Noah took a few steps forward, getting as close to the edge of the bed as he dared. He looked down at the hundreds of adoring pink faces as they stood waiting for him to address them. There was an awed silence.

This is what power, real power, feels like, Noah thought. He knew they wanted him to speak, but he didn't know what to say. Noah didn't want to sound stupid, and he didn't want to sound like a kid. He wanted to sound like a leader, eloquent, yet commanding.

I guess the Commander is right, he thought. I've always been their leader. I've been commanding them for most of my life. His face suddenly brightened. I can do this. I can do this, he reassured himself. Then Noah took a deep breath and called down as loud as he could, "Hi, guys!"

Hundreds of little hands clapped at the sound of Noah's voice.

"I . . . uh . . . want you all to know," Noah continued, "that I am still your leader." Another round of applause followed this. "I'd also like to say that Crunch has done a great job, and I want him to continue as my second-in-command." Soon little pink arms were raised, waving wildly in the air. Noah couldn't help but enjoy the moment. He felt like a rock star entertaining his fans or like a king addressing his subjects. He knew that they would do anything for him. They loved him without question. In fact the little wrestlers were so concerned for his safety, that under Crunch's supervision, they were climbing up onto one another's shoulders. In no time, they had formed a ladder of bodies that went from the rug up the side of the bed.

The last man to start climbing was Crunch. He made his way to the wrestler on top, then grabbed the blanket and jumped on the bed with a grunt. He bowed his head as he approached Noah.

"Noah, sir," he squeaked, "we're at your service night and day. And I'd just like to say," he closed his eyes tight, trying to concentrate on his rhyme, "if you need to come down, it's a long way to the ground. But we'll get you there safe and sound. Our backs are strong, our hearts are true. We love you, and cauliflower, too."

Before Noah was able to reply, Gordy put

his hand on Crunch's head. "Little Crunch, you're the best of the bunch." Gordy laughed. The Commander shook his head, and Nate and Noah giggled. Then Noah stuck out his hand.

"Thanks, Crunch. Gordy's right. You are the best." He shook the puffy pink hand. (Crunch even had muscles popping up on his fingers.)

Noah turned to the Commander. "I guess we can't stay in bed all day."

"I'd say naptime is officially over," the Commander replied. He turned and grabbed the shoulders of the topmost wrestler, and began the climb down. Gordy quickly followed. Nate stood staring at the wobbly ladder of little pink bodies that was swaying back and forth.

"It sure is a long way to the ground," he whispered to Noah.

"I know," Noah said. "I guess we have to think of it like the ropes in gym."

"Right," Nate replied, taking a few steps back. Crunch came up beside him.

"If you like, you can follow me," Crunch

said shyly. "It's as simple as climbing down a tree. Don't look at the ground, it will only make you frown. Keep your eye on me and you'll see how easy it can be." He reached out and patted Nate's knee, for he wasn't much taller than that. Nate looked over at Noah and tried to smile.

"OK, little guy," he said, "we'll be right behind you."

Noah waited for Nate to start down and then grabbed the top wrestler. Slowly he made his way over the wobbly pink bodies, following the others. When he reached the rug, the crowd went wild. Noah blushed with pleasure.

"That Crunch sure is brave for being so tiny. It was kind of scary there for a while, but I guess we can breathe easier now that we're on the ground," Nate whispered to Noah and Gordy.

"Um," Gordy mumbled, reaching for another piece of bubble gum stashed in his pocket. "What's there to be afraid of down here?" Suddenly, as if in answer to his question, a bloodcurdling cry filled the air. Everyone turned in the direction of the sound.

"What the heck is that!" Nate whispered as a giant lime-green mass appeared on the other side of the orange bathrobe lying on the floor.

"Oh, no!" Noah cried. "It can't be. It just can't . . ." But before he could say another word, the giant green mass turned around and with a thunderous roar, opened its blood-red mouth and spit out a piece of banana.

"Oh, my gosh!" Gordy whispered. "It looks like . . . like . . ."

"Like an AckAck!" Noah gasped.

CHAPTER NINE

"AckAck?" Gordy repeated. "What is an AckAck?"

"It's my little cousin Jack's toy monster," Noah whispered, as AckAck let out another roar.

"Noah, maybe you haven't noticed, but that monster over there is no toy," Gordy replied. "That big ugly thing is alive!"

Noah winced at the sight of the howling beast. It stood on two legs. Its long scaly neck was twisting this way and that from its massive green torso. Its head was small, covered with green and brown warts. Dark-green, crusty eyelids drooped over two gigantic bloodshot eyeballs. Its mouth was

76

large and flapping, with a set of fanglike
teeth that seemed to be grinding continu-
ously. The beast's bloodcurdling howl was
somewhere between a scream and a roar. It
was the most frightening thing Noah had
ever seen, even in his nightmares!

"I must have blown some of the magic
powder on him when I sneezed," Nate
gasped.

"Didn't your mother teach you to hold
your hand over your mouth?" Gordy whispered.

The monster's horrible bloodshot eyes
rolled in their direction. "Oh, no," Nate
cried. "He sees us!"

"He must have picked up our scent," the
Commander said, taking a step back.

"It's those darn little wrestlers." Gordy
groaned. "They're so sweaty, he could probably smell them all the way to Kansas!"

"Now, Gordy, don't be rude. The little
fellows helped us get down from the bed.
They were there when we needed them,"
the Commander reminded him.

Noah looked at Crunch and his fellow

wrestlers. They were all huddled together, their muscles taut with terror. They seemed to be waiting, expecting some kind of orders.

The Commander put his hand on Noah's shoulder. "Just concentrate on outsmarting the beast," the Commander told him, nodding to AckAck. "Don't dwell on what you can't accomplish or you'll never accomplish anything."

"Right, Commander," Noah said. He looked up at AckAck and cringed. "It's just that he's so big," Noah whispered.

"This creature has got a big body but you've got a big brain. All you have to do is use it, old friend," the Commander told him.

Noah shook his head. He loved it when the Commander called him "old friend." Everyone stood staring as AckAck began to swing his head from left to right, opening and closing his mouth. Suddenly the beast began moving forward.

"Quick, under the bed!" Noah yelled. "We can hide under there until we can think of a plan." The Commander, Gordy, and Nate all

ran after Noah as he dove for cover.
Crunch and his men followed right behind
them. Once they were safely hidden behind a few shoe boxes, Noah called to the
wrestlers to halt. Crunch signaled for his
men to form into lines. Then, on Crunch's
command, they sat down in place to rest.
Meanwhile, Noah, Nate, the Commander,
and Gordy leaned against a shoe box,
catching their breath.

"If only there were some way that we
could distract AckAck," Nate said.

"Shh, listen," Noah whispered. "Did you
hear that?" Everyone sat listening to a series
of low grumbles that soon developed into a
full-blown bark.

"It's Overdue!" Noah cried. "I'd know that
bark anywhere." Overdue's bark was followed by a loud screech from AckAck, as he
dashed toward the wastebasket and dove behind it.

Overdue came running into the room. He
got down on his front paws and whined as he
tried to get his nose behind the wastebasket.
Noah could see his tail wagging back and

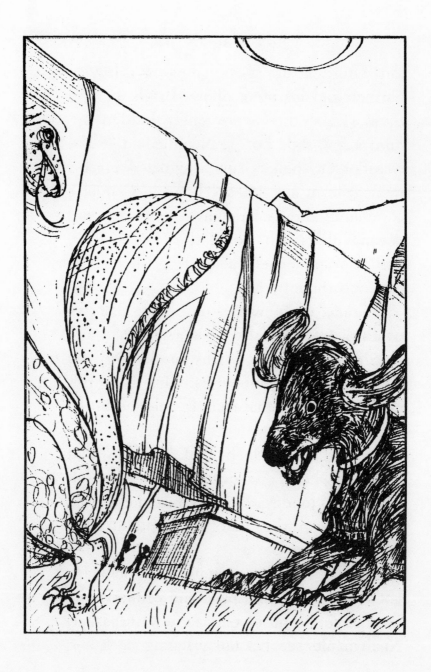

forth excitedly. "He'll never be able to budge that wastebasket," said Noah. "It's filled with rocks."

"Good," said the Commander. "We can count on Overdue to keep AckAck busy for a while."

"We can count on him as long as my mom doesn't walk by my bedroom," Noah told them. "If she sees Overdue here, she'll send him downstairs. He's not allowed upstairs without me or Jess."

"Let's just hope she doesn't walk by," Gordy said. "We need this time to figure out a line of attack."

"Attack?" Nate cried. He turned to Noah. "You've got to stop this now or someone could get hurt. That monster is real and he could kill us. I'd eat all of Allison's meatless meat loaf rather than have to face that thing. You've got to undo the wish!"

"I can't undo the wish," Noah tried to explain.

"What do you mean you can't undo it?" Nate shouted. "You got us into this mess, now you have to get us out!"

Noah could see the fear in his best friend's eyes. He could hear it in his voice. Noah recognized the terror that Nate was experiencing, for it was the same terror that he was feeling himself.

"I'm sorry, Nate," Noah said, trying not to cry. "I didn't know all this was going to happen. I didn't think the magic powder was going to fall on AckAck, and it wouldn't have if you hadn't sneezed."

"You can't blame this on me," Nate snapped.

"Hold it, you two," the Commander interrupted. "No one is to blame here. And if you waste your time arguing, we'll never come up with a plan to attack the beast."

"The Commander's right," Gordy added. "So just what does this meatless meat loaf taste like?"

"Gordy, not now." The Commander sighed.

"Oh, right," Gordy muttered. "I guess you can tell me about it another time." He put his hand on Nate's shoulder. "Don't worry, little buddy, things may seem tough now,

but the big C and I have been through missions that were a lot worse than this. We've
had some real hair-raisers, right, Commander?" Gordy flashed his gap-toothed grin.
"Do you remember the time last year when
that mouse Ben Franklin was chasing us in
your classroom?"

"That was a hamster, Gordy," Noah cor-
rected him. "And his name wasn't Ben
Franklin. It was George Washington."

"George Washington, Ben Franklin,
whatever that ridiculous rodent's name was,
I'll never forget that chase. He ate up half of
my shirt!" Gordy frowned. "This shirt was a
real fashion statement at one time, I can tell
you." He ran his fingers over the front of his
shirt. It was bright orange with green palm
trees and coconuts. The back had been completely ripped off by the hamster. Nate and
Noah looked over at what was left of Gordy's
gaudy coconut shirt.

"Gordy saved my life on that mission. It
took real courage to distract that hamster the
way he did," the Commander said with a
nod.

"Aw, shucks, Commander." Gordy ran his hand through his wavy red hair. "It wasn't courage. I just wanted to see how fast that fat furball could run." Everyone laughed, and Noah turned to Nate.

"We're going to be all right, Nate, really, we are," Noah said.

"Sure," Gordy added. "We're a team. We're . . . we're . . ." Suddenly his voice grew shaky. "We're not alone!" He gulped, pointing in the direction of one of the shoe boxes. Everyone followed his gaze. They fell silent as they sat staring at a green machine gun that was aimed at them.

Suddenly from behind the other shoe boxes hundreds of green guns appeared. Noah tried to see who was holding the weapons, but whoever they were had taken cover behind the shoe boxes. Only hundreds of hands were exposed, as they clutched the guns.

"Oh, my gosh!" Nate cried. "Look at those hands! They're . . . green!"

"Could they be your aliens, Noah?" the

Commander asked, nervously eyeing all the weaponry. "The aliens were green, weren't they?"

"Yes, but only some of them," Noah replied. "Most of the others were blue. And none of them had conventional weapons. Only my army men have guns like that. But, oh, no, I just remembered," his voice trailed off.

"Remembered what?" Nate whispered.

"My box of army men was open and just below the bed when you sneezed. The magic powder must have fallen on them, too," Noah told him.

Nate groaned. Suddenly a figure appeared from behind a box. He was in complete formal military dress, and looked like a high-ranking officer in the United States Army, except that he was green from head to toe. Even his eyelashes were green.

"The General!" Noah gasped. "It's General Meatball!" Noah and the others gazed at the figure before them. He was standing a good distance away, surveying the situation.

"General Meatball? How did you ever come up with a name like that?" Nate whispered.

"Well, I just called him General until Overdue carried him off one day. I finally found him in Overdue's dog dish. He was lying underneath a leftover meatball," Noah explained. "People only make fun of his name before they get to know him. They stop laughing once they realize what a smart and brave soldier he is."

"Whew, I'm glad Overdue never got an urge to carry me off," Gordy said. "Just think, I could have been stuck with a beaut of a name like Beef Chunk or Spaghetti Mold!"

"Shh, Gordy, not now," the Commander whispered. "General Meatball is coming this way."

CHAPTER TEN

Noah and the others stood staring as General Meatball approached. Behind him, an army of green soldiers followed. Crunch and his men had gotten to their feet and stood nervously waiting. It was a tense moment, as the two groups eyed each other silently.

The little wrestlers, pink and full of shiny muscles, looked menacing. The army men, green and carrying weapons, looked fierce. The army men tightened their fingers on the triggers of their guns. The wrestlers puffed out their chests and flexed their muscles. Even Crunch's earlobes quivered. Finally the General walked up to Gordy and cleared his throat.

"I am General Putnam T. Meatball, United States Army," he said. Gordy grinned and saluted. Then he blew a bubble that was so big it touched the General's nose. The General seemed confused and quickly backed away. Before Noah could say anything, the General had gone up to Crunch, who was standing before his group of wrestlers.

"I am General Putnam T. Meatball, United States Army," the General repeated. The wrestlers suddenly fell over each other laughing. The army men gritted their teeth, waiting for the laughter to die down. Noah could see how hard it was for the soldiers, especially the new recruits. They shook with anger, looking at the wrestlers and then back at their leader. But General Meatball's face was a mask of serenity. The troops regained their composure.

"I see you little fellows are easily amused," the General said, standing tall. Noah was glad that he had put the General's field boots

on him. They made him took taller. He tow-
ered over Crunch, who just reached his
waist. Crunch took a step forward, warily
eyeing the weapons pointing in his direction.

"I am second-in-command of this bunch,
and you can call me Crunch," he rhymed
proudly. The army men quickly lowered
their weapons and held their sides with
laughter. When the wrestlers realized that
they were being laughed at, they locked
arms without so much as a word passing
among them, and began to advance.

Noah held out his arm. "Stop!" he ordered. The wrestlers came to a halt. Noah
nodded at the General. "I'm your leader,"
he told him. The General stared blankly, not
recognizing him. "It's me, Noah," he cried.

"Noah?" The General gasped. "But it can't
be!"

"Yes, it can." Noah smiled. "I guess I'm
going to be your size, for a little while, any-
way," he explained. The General stood
blinking, then turned to his troops.

"Attention!" he bellowed. The army men

stood stock-still and then proceeded to salute. "Noah, sir!" The General saluted, turning to his leader. "At your service, sir!"

"Overdue, what are you doing up here?" Mrs. Murphy's voice suddenly boomed. "Come on, Due, let's go downstairs now." Noah froze as he and the others stood listening. They could hear Mrs. Murphy's footsteps and Overdue's unhappy whine.

"That's enough of that," Mrs. Murphy said firmly, entering the room. "Come on, let's go." She grabbed Overdue's collar and pulled him across the floor and out the door. The room was filled with a deadly silence, only to be broken by the thump of AckAck's tail as he left his hiding place and made his way across the room toward the bed.

"The situation is this," Noah began, his voice cracking with fear. "There is a beast called AckAck. He's part dinosaur and part monster, and he's on the loose." AckAck let out a scream. "That's him," Noah added nervously.

"Sounds like he's closing in." Nate winced.

"Nate's right!" Gordy cried. "Look!" He pointed to an ugly head with two bloodshot eyes that were at the same low level as he was, only a few feet from the end of the bed.

"He's going to try crawling under the bed! Oh, no!" Noah yelled. "Commander, I don't know what to do!"

"Just stay calm, Noah," the Commander told him.

Stay calm! Noah thought. How can anyone stay calm with that thing on the loose. I don't want to be a leader. I don't want to be in charge. I just want to run as far away as I can! But he knew that everyone was depending on him. He could see the wrestlers flexing their muscles and the army men gripping their guns. They looked at Noah, waiting for him to tell them what to do. He took a deep breath and cleared his throat.

"General Meatball," Noah called, "have your men fire on the beast at once."

"Yes, sir." The General saluted. "We'll bring him down. Don't you worry, sir." He turned to his men, and directed them into a line. The army men tightened their green grips on their green guns. They stood tensely waiting for the order to fire. Everyone seemed to be holding his breath as the loud rumblings from the monster's empty stomach filled the air.

"Ready, aim, fire!" the General shouted. Noah closed his eyes, prepared to hear the blast of guns going off. There was a loud clicking noise in the air as hundreds of soldiers pulled their triggers, but the accompanying sound of gunfire never came. Noah opened his eyes. The guns weren't loaded! Now AckAck's nose was under the bed.

The General rushed up to Noah. "It's the darnedest thing, sir. I've never seen anything like it. The beast is totally unharmed by our attack," he reported.

"Well, of course he's unharmed," Noah told him. "You haven't fired any bullets at him!"

"Bullets, sir?" The General looked confused.

"Bullets," Nate repeated. "You know, the little hard things that come out of guns when you shoot them."

The General fidgeted uncomfortably and finally admitted, "We . . . er . . . don't seem to have any bullets, sir."

"But you have so many guns, why don't you have bullets?" Noah wanted to know.

The Commander suddenly took Noah aside. "This is an embarrassing situation for the General," the Commander whispered. "You must remember that he and his men have never been anything but toy soldiers with toy guns. And toy guns don't usually come with bullets."

"I guess not," Noah mumbled. His shoulders slumped as he surveyed the hundreds of useless guns that the army men were holding. He heard Gordy begin to whistle. Gordy always whistled when he was nervous, and there was a good deal to be nervous about. The beast was opening his bloodstained mouth, displaying his sharp fanglike teeth. A wave of hot rancid air blew over them as AckAck exhaled. His long scaly neck slowly began twisting its way farther under the bed. The rumble of his empty stomach echoed in their ears.

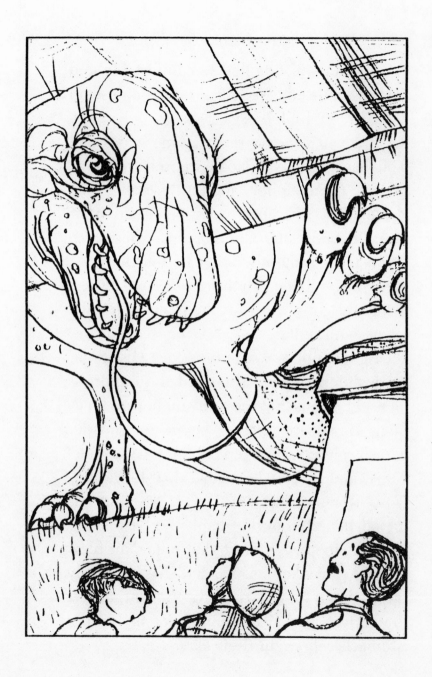

"Look! He's so big that he's gotten stuck!" Noah yelled. Everyone stood staring at the mighty beast, who threw his head from side to side as he tried to wrench free.

"It won't be long before he gets himself loose and then he'll be after us again," Nate whispered.

"We don't even have any weapons to use against him," Noah moaned.

"Guns and bullets don't give you power," the Commander said. "They're just tools— and tools of destruction at that. I'm always telling Gordy to use positive thinking. Dwell on the good and the good will be there for you. Think one good thought and another is sure to follow." AckAck howled loudly as he twisted his neck to look in their direction.

"I don't know, Commander," Gordy whispered. "It sure is hard to be thinking good thoughts when you are looking at that ugly face."

"Quick, Noah, we better move everyone out and find some safe shelter," the Commander said.

"Shelter, right," Noah replied, looking

around. "Where can we find shelter?" His face suddenly brightened.

"Nate," Noah cried, "the space station! We can take shelter there."

"Great idea," Nate said, giving Noah the thumbs-up. Noah turned to the crowd before him. "The space station should offer excellent shelter," he told them. "It's got complete defense and offense capability."

"Noah, sir, we know we can depend on you to see us through," Crunch called out. The wrestlers cheered.

The General turned to his men. "Men," he bellowed, "we're about to witness some of the most modern assault weaponry known to man." The army men waved their guns and cheered. The General turned to face Noah. "Just what are we talking about here, sir?" the General asked. "Sonar bombing?"

Noah looked at the crowd of anxious pink and green faces before him. He frowned and shook his head.

"Well, not exactly," he said.

"I know." The General smiled. "Photon cannons?"

Noah shook his head again. "Not quite," he said with a wince.

"Radioactive sensitizers?" the General tried once more. A hush came over the crowd as the soldiers and wrestlers anxiously waited for their leader to reply. Noah coughed, cleared his throat, and gulped.

"Actually, it's catapults and marbles," he said in a little voice.

CHAPTER ELEVEN

Noah ran for the space station, with everyone following close behind. The beast was wailing loudly now as he struggled to break loose. The sight and smell of all the little figures racing before him gave AckAck the strength he needed to finally squeeze free. He howled with delight and began to chase the little figures.

Noah looked back to see all the army men and the wrestlers behind him. "How are you doing?" Noah called to Nate.

"I'm thinking good thoughts, but I'm hearing some bad sounds above me!" Nate yelled back. Suddenly Nate tripped and fell. The great beast swooped down and curled his long wet tongue around Nate's leg. Noah watched with horror as the monster dragged his friend across the floor.

"Help! Help!" Nate screamed. Noah ran alongside him, trying to pry him free, but the monster's strong tongue was more than he could contend with. Suddenly Gordy reached into his pack and took out a large chunk of bubble gum. He threw it to Nate, telling him to place it on the tip of AckAck's tongue. When the beast tasted the sweet gum, he relaxed his tongue for just a second and Nate fell to the floor.

"Gordy, you saved my life!" Nate gasped, as Gordy and the Commander helped him to his feet. Noah turned around to see AckAck gobbling up the gum. Then the beast bent down over a shoe box full of superheroes. His bloodshot eyes rolled about, searching the contents of the box for something else to eat.

"I wish that some of the magic powder had fallen on my superheroes," Noah said.

"Oh, please, don't ever mention magic powder again," Nate cried.

"The wrestlers and the army men are right

behind us," Gordy said. "How far is it to the space station?"

"It's just around the corner at the foot of my bed," Noah told him.

"It won't be long before AckAck loses interest in those shoe boxes," the Commander warned. "We'd better keep moving." They all took off for the foot of the bed and turned the corner, coming upon the outer wall of the station.

Noah and Nate stopped and stared wide-eyed at the mass of gray rock that stretched as far as they could see.

"Wow!" Nate cried. "It's our rock wall! Let's find the tunnel that leads to the other side." The little group clamored through the opening. As Noah came out in front of the space station, he stood speechless. The interlocking plastic blocks of red, blue, and yellow rose up in a feast of color. Instrument panels gleamed on each level, as lights flashed and computers hummed.

"It's beautiful!" Nate sighed.

"It's . . . it's real!" Noah marveled.

"Some of the magic powder must have

fallen on it," the Commander observed. Soon Noah and the others were surrounded by the army men and wrestlers who had followed them through the passageway.

AckAck was in hot pursuit. Noah could feel the goose bumps breaking out on his skin as he listened to the monster's angry cries.

"Quick, everybody," he shouted, "inside the station, hurry!" Hundreds of wrestlers and army men began to run in formation as Noah and Nate directed them into the station.

Once inside, Noah and the Commander conferred with Crunch and the General. "This station is outfitted with ten catapults and a full supply of marbles," Noah told them. "It's the best way we have of defending ourselves."

"Why don't we position the General's men at the catapults, since they're tall enough to operate them?" the Commander suggested.

"Good thinking, Commander," Noah agreed. "And Crunch, since your men are the strongest, they should relay the marbles from the ammunition room to the outer walkway. Begin the relay of marbles immediately, but don't release the catapults until I've given the order. And remember," Noah said, turning his head to look out of the large windows, "AckAck is not going to rest until he has knocked down that rock wall, and once he has, we must be ready for him."

Crunch and the General sprang into action, directing their men to regroup. Soon the pounding of hundreds of feet could be heard as green and pink men alike raced along the walkways.

Noah and the Commander joined Gordy and Nate, who were admiring Jess's instrument panels on the walls of the lower level. There were computer screens, scanning screens, and map panels for intergalactic travel. The walls were lit with a soft blue light. Symbols and numbers flashed on the different screens in a rainbow of color.

"Look," Nate gasped, "Jess's instrument panel really works!"

"It's too bad that he can't be here to see

this," Noah sighed, touching a brightly lit screen. "He'd love to see what the space station looks like now."

"But I don't think he'd like to see what AckAck looks like now," Nate said. "Wow!" he exclaimed. "Look at this intergalactic mapping device. This station has everything!"

"Everything but a refrigerator," Gordy complained. "Why is it that when kids build these things, they never put in refrigerators? I could really go for a little snack right now."

"Good grief, Gordy," said the Commander, "how can you be thinking of snacks at a time like this?"

"I'm not the only one who's thinking of his stomach," Gordy said, his voice quivering as he pointed to the station's large windows. Noah followed his gaze to see AckAck's hulking frame approaching. The sounds of crashing rocks filled the air.

"He's come through the rock wall!" Nate cried.

"Let's get upstairs to the walkway!" Noah

shouted. "The catapults should be loaded with the first round of marbles by now."

When the four reached the upper level, they found long lines of sweaty wrestlers stretching from the ammunition room to the catapults. Each wrestler was standing with feet apart and arms lowered as he held the weighty marbles. The little pink muscles on the wrestler's arms glistened with sweat.

"Whew!" Gordy whispered, holding his nose. "Somebody could do a deodorant commercial up here. You know, a Before-and-After thing. These little guys could definitely be the Before."

"They may not smell all that great," Noah pointed out, "but they sure are getting the job done." He looked over to see the army men adjusting the catapult merchanisms. Each catapult was loaded and ready to go.

"Rrrrrr . . ." A ferocious roar was followed by an avalanche of rock. AckAck was towering above them.

Beneath the monster's shadow, Noah's legs felt weak and his stomach ached. Why

did I think I'd be brave enough to lead everybody? he wondered. All I really want to do is run and hide!

Noah looked at the anxious pink and green faces that surrounded him. Somehow he would have to find the courage to lead an attack. Noah took a deep breath. "Ready, aim, fire!" he cried.

CHAPTER TWELVE

The army men released the catapults as the wrestlers cheered. The colored marbles went flying through the air, pelting AckAck's chest. The beast angrily swung his head around.

"It worked! It worked!" Gordy cried as they stood watching the bewildered monster take a step backward.

"Keep loading the catapults!" Noah shouted. Crunch directed his men to relay more of the marbles, and in a few seconds the catapults were reloaded and ready to fire. Noah looked at the army men, who stood waiting for his command. "Ready, aim, fire!" he shouted. The beast was again pummeled with the flying missiles. AckAck opened his mouth in an angry cry.

"Direct hit!" Nate exclaimed. A volley of marbles had shot straight into the creature's mouth. Everyone stood watching as the beast closed first his mouth and then his eyes. AckAck's mighty jaws began to move slowly in a chewing motion. Suddenly the crusted green eyelids lifted, the monster's mouth opened slightly, and he spit out the broken pieces of marble.

"Oh, my gosh," Nate whispered, "he chewed up those marbles as if they were so many peanuts!"

"Just think how fast he could chew up one of us." Gordy shuddered.

"Fire! Fire! Fire!" Noah called out repeatedly. The wrestlers groaned under the weight of the marbles, while the army men were busy positioning the catapults. As Ack-Ack tried to walk toward the station, he began to slip and slide on the marbles that littered the floor. The beast howled loudly, unable to keep his balance.

"Come on, big boy, you can do better than that," Gordy taunted. AckAck's eyes narrowed, becoming two green slits as he lifted his foot carefully, only to put it down on still more marbles. A hushed silence fell over the space station as everyone stood watching the mighty AckAck go slipping and sliding across the floor. He finally fell over backward, hitting his head on the toy box.

"He's down!" Noah yelled. "We brought him down!" They stood staring at the hulking mass of green monster that lay on the floor. Everyone cheered and laughed.

"Do you think he's dead?" Nate wondered aloud.

"He's either dead or knocked out," Gordy said. "Either way, the big boy is definitely down and out for the count." But as hundreds of cheers went up all over the space station, and wrestlers and army men embraced, a large crusted eyelid was slowly opening. A huge bloodshot eyeball silently surveyed the scene.

"Oh, no!" Noah moaned. "Look, he's up

again!" The monster had found a path across the floor that was clear of marbles and he was slowly making his way toward them.

"We don't have much ammunition left. We've got to come up with a plan to distract him, or that monster will tear down this whole station," the Commander said. Everyone stood shuddering at the horrifying sight before them.

"I think it would take a lot to distract Ack-Ack now," Gordy whispered.

"The Zoomlor!" Noah shouted. "It would take the Zoomlor!"

"What are you talking about, Noah?" Nate asked nervously.

"We can distract AckAck with the Zoomlor," Noah told him. "It's parked right down on the launchpad. Once the four of us start flying it, we can get AckAck to follow us. Meanwhile, the army men and wrestlers will have a chance to escape."

"Fly? You want to fly in the Zoomlor? But it's not a real spaceship," cried Nate.

"It's as real as the space station," the Commander pointed out. "And presumably the magic dust fell on it when it showered down on the space station."

"If we're going to do anything, we'd better do it now!" Gordy shouted above the angry roars of the beast.

"Quick," Noah yelled, "let's run for the launchpad!" He raced down the walkway with the Commander, Nate, and Gordy following close behind.

Crash! Bang! Crash! AckAck was trying to grab the space station. He pulled down a catapult and stuck it in his mouth. Then he spit it out, making a face.

Noah grabbed Nate's arm and the two ran the last few inches to the launchpad. They stopped and stood staring at the gleaming spaceship before them. The landing gear was down and the loading ramp was in place. The Zoomlor was ready and waiting for takeoff. It was the most detailed spacecraft that Noah and Jess had ever built. Gordy and the Commander came up beside them. Nate's mouth dropped open.

"Wow, what a ship," he whispered. The magnificent machine's engines were softly purring, and the outer deck lights were glowing an iridescent green. The ship's sleek purple body was decorated with silver swirls, and the cabin lights glowed through the clear dome top.

"Now all we have to do is get her in the air," Noah said, as they raced up the loading ramp and into the cabin.

CHAPTER THIRTEEN

Once inside the Zoomlor, they tried closing the doors, but gave up when they realized that everything was automated.

"I wish that Jess were here," Noah moaned. "He designed all the instrument panels for the ship. He would know how to work everything."

"Where's the refrigerator?" Gordy wanted to know. He began searching the cabin.

"Look!" Noah cried, walking over to the monitoring screen. "AckAck is about to rip off the roof of the station! We've got to figure out how to get this thing airborne." He lowered himself into a silver-cushioned seat before the control panels.

"I'm afraid that I don't know much about these computerized machines," the Commander said, staring at the maze of dials and buttons on the instrument panel.

"I thought you went on a lot of air patrols for Noah," Nate said, sitting down beside him.

"Those were prop planes," the Commander told him. "Gordy and I are a couple of old-timers. We're used to roughing it."

"The Commander and Gordy were having too many adventures to get trained for space flights," Noah said. "That's why I'm glad you're here."

"Me?" Nate squeaked. "Why are you glad that I'm here?"

"Because you're the only one who can fly this thing," Noah told him. Everyone jumped at the sound of AckAck's tail hitting the station. He was just inches away now.

"But I don't know how to fly this thing!" Nate gasped.

"What do you mean you don't know how to fly it?" Noah cried. "What was all that stuff about being champion of Air Patrol? And flying blindfolded?"

"I am champion when it comes to video flight," Nate stammered. "But this is real life! We could really crash in this thing!"

"The only crashing going on right now is over there," Gordy said, pointing in Ack-Ack's direction. Noah and Nate looked out of the Zoomlor to see AckAck pulling down the space station's lookout towers. With a deafening roar, the hungry beast proceeded to smash the towers against the rock wall. Hundreds of trembling pink and green faces were pressed against the station's windows, watching the mighty monster's attack.

"Nate, remember, Crunch and his men were there for us. We can't let them down now," Noah said solemnly.

Nate stared at the instrument panel. "I wonder if it's all that different from playing a video game," he mumbled, pushing a blue button. A computer lit up and a series of commands appeared on the screen. LIFT

RAMP was the first command. CLOSE DOORS was the second.

"It may be as easy as playing Air Patrol," Nate whispered. "Just maybe I can do this," he said, pulling down a lever. The ramp began to rise and the doors slid closed. Suddenly a gigantic green bloodshot eyeball was peering through the clear dome top.

"Quick, Nate! Get her up!" Noah cried. Nate pushed a small red button. Everyone was thrown back in his seat as the engines roared and the ship lifted off the ground.

"Nate, you did it!" Noah cried. "We're in the air!"

"This must be the steering device," Nate sang out happily. He pulled a joystick to the right, and the ship suddenly veered right, flying out of AckAck's confused reach.

"That's it!" Gordy yelled. "You've got it figured out!" Nate moved the lever up, and the ship flew upward.

"I don't believe this," Noah cried. "I'm flying in the Zoomlor with Nate at the controls!"

"He does seem to have a natural flair for flying." The Commander smiled. Noah pressed his nose to the dome and looked below.

"It's a good thing you decided to come along on this adventure, Nate, or we'd still be down there," Noah whispered. AckAck was staring up at them, a bewildered expression on his ugly monster face.

"Captain of Air Patrol at your service," Nate grinned. "We've got his attention now. Which way should we go? How about over by the windows?" The ship jerked as the Zoomlor sped toward the ceiling.

"Wrong way! You're going the wrong way!" Noah screamed. Nate pushed the lever down, just as they were about to crash into the light fixture. They sighed with relief as the ship righted itself and flew around the bedroom. AckAck was trying to follow, having forgotten all about the space station.

"Sorry, wrong lever," Nate said in a small voice. He steered the ship to the left and brought them down, just above the floor.

Noah was feeling green, as if he were going to throw up. He held his hands over his mouth and let out a low moan.

"Are you going to be sick?" Nate asked. "You sure look like you could use an airsickness container."

Noah groaned.

"My cousin Alex ate four packs of peanuts and a bunch of Cheeze Whiz on a plane," Nate continued. "When he started to throw up, the flight attendant gave him this bag that said 'airsickness container.' When he threw up, some of it landed on his leg. He had to ask the flight attendant for a napkin. He told her that some of his 'airsickness' missed the container!"

"Nate, will you stop talking about airsickness!" Noah cried. He shut his mouth tight, determined not to give in to the queasy feeling that was overtaking him. "I'll be OK," he said through clenched teeth. "I'm just a little . . ."

"Nate! Look out!" Noah suddenly yelled. "You're flying straight for him!"

Nate looked up. AckAck was dead ahead, just inches away. Nate desperately tried to find a button for reverse but couldn't. They were flying so close to the floor that AckAck reached down and picked up the Zoomlor. He began to shake it.

Inside the ship's cabin, everyone was thrown out of his seat. AckAck howled with frustration as he tried to reach the little figures inside.

"Oh . . . oh . . . oh, no!" everyone was screaming in the cabin. The powerful beast raised the ship in the air and was about to dash it against the wall. Noah closed his eyes tight and grabbed Nate, expecting the worst, when he suddenly heard a loud voice, louder than AckAck's screams.

"Ba . . . ba . . . bad AckAck!" Jack's voice boomed. AckAck's ferocious howls turned to a soft purring at the sound of his owner's scolding. The monster let go of the spaceship. The Zoomlor automatically resumed its course, flying around the bedroom.

"Look! It's my little cousin Jack!" Noah exclaimed, getting back into his seat.

CHAPTER FOURTEEN

The crew of the Zoomlor peered down to
see the smiling, curly-haired toddler standing on the rug below. He was dressed in
little green overalls and a T-shirt that had a
picture of Frankenstein on the front.

"It looks like Jack just escaped," Noah told
the others. "My mom must be cleaning upstairs. He loves to come in here when he's
not supposed to. Mom is probably looking
for him right now." Everyone watched as
the toddler took a step toward the beast.
AckAck's long leathery tongue curled out of
his mouth as he stood licking his lips.

"Oh, no!" Noah gasped. Jack took another
step toward AckAck and held out his hand.

"We've got to stop him! Jack could get hurt!" But to Noah's surprise the beast bowed his head and meekly licked the little out-stretched hand. Jack was delighted with his now real-live AckAck. He threw back his head and began to laugh. Then he bent down and gave his monster a big sloppy kiss.

AckAck groaned and ran across the room to hide.

"I guess monsters hate to be kissed," said Noah. He looked down to see AckAck peeking out from behind the wastepaper basket.

"Great," Gordy whispered. "The next time he tries to eat us, we can just blow him a kiss."

Nate steered the ship to the left and everyone looked down at Jack. "He's a cute little guy," the Commander said, waving to the baby below. Jack smiled and waved at the ship. Then he stretched out his arms and tried to grab it. When he couldn't reach the ship, he picked up a block from the floor and threw it, just missing the Zoomlor by inches.

"Hey! Cut that out!" Gordy cried, shaking his finger at the laughing toddler. Jack picked up two more blocks and hurled them in the air.

"Jack the Maniac is more dangerous than any old monster," Noah said. Nate tried to steer the ship to the other side of the room. Jack laughed and picked up the hairbrush from the floor. He lifted his arm to throw it, but stopped suddenly and blinked at the sight before him. Hundreds of tiny pink and green men were pouring out of the space station.

"Look, it's the guys!" Noah said, pointing down to the stream of army men and wrestlers that were now running toward the bed.

"AckAck is on the attack again," Gordy whispered. The beast was howling as he came out from behind the wastebasket and chased after the little figures. The army men and wrestlers were racing frantically, trying to escape. They hadn't gone far, however, when they ran straight into Jack. The baby stood dumbfounded at the sight of all the little pink and green men. His small lips curled into a perfect O. He tilted his head as he stood staring.

The General was so confused about his men's position that he ordered them to "Climb!" Suddenly Jack's white baby shoe was covered with little olive green men. They swarmed over the laces and then dove into the cuff of Jack's overalls. Meanwhile AckAck roared and started pawing the air with his arms. Jack paid no attention to his monster now. He reached down for the tiny pink and green men and began to giggle as they squirmed out of his grasp.

"Oh, no!" Noah cried. "Look, he's got Crunch!" Crunch was trying to slide out of Jack's grasp, back down into the safety of his pants cuff. Jack held up the tiny wrestler close to his face. Then he slowly opened his mouth.

"We've got to distract Jack before he swallows Crunch!" Noah yelled. Nate pulled on the joystick and guided the ship over to the bed. Jack was standing a few inches away. The baby looked at the Zoomlor as it hovered above Noah's pillow. He closed his mouth and smiled. Then he took a step toward the bed and held out his hand. Crunch tumbled down to the rug below. He quickly jumped up and joined the General in directing the men to evacuate.

"Let's take off before he gets any closer," Gordy said, nervously eyeing Jack's approach.

"We've got to wait for Crunch and the General to get their men to safety," the Commander said. They watched as the wrestlers and army men raced under the bed to hide. Jack took a step closer to the bed.

"We'd better take her up before Jack gets any closer!" cried Noah.

"I can't!" Nate exclaimed. "The lift-off lever is stuck!" The toddler was towering over them. Gordy and the Commander frantically tried to pull on the lever, but it wouldn't budge. A horrible drumming noise filled the cabin, as a huge baby finger began tapping on the ship's dome. A big blue eyeball suddenly appeared, scanning the contents of the cabin.

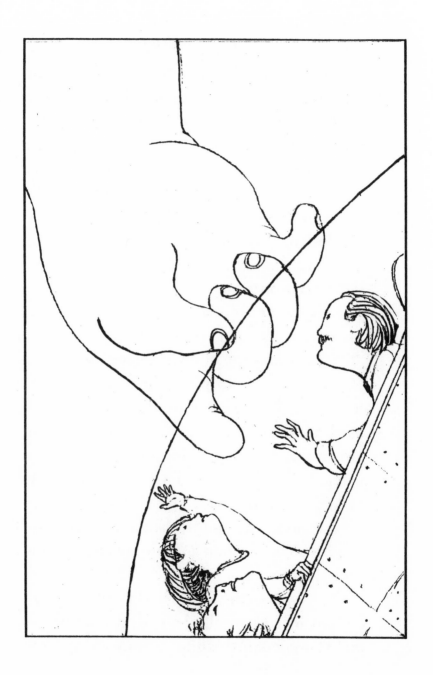

"No-No! No-No!" the baby called, as he recognized Noah. He grabbed at the ship with one hand, while reaching for the hairbrush on the rug with the other. He held the brush up, as if to smash it against the ship.

"Down, Jack! Put the hairbrush down!" Noah shouted as loud as he could.

"No-No, No-No," Jack happily sang, swinging the hairbrush. Suddenly the bedroom door opened.

"Jack, what are you doing in here?" Mrs. Murphy exclaimed, coming into the room. "I've been looking all over for you. Oh, no, Jack, you're not to play with the big boys' toys!" she scolded, taking the ship and the hairbrush from his hands. Since she was a grown-up, Mrs. Murphy couldn't see the magic before her eyes. To her, the Zoomlor looked like a toy with four little plastic figures inside. She gently laid the spaceship and brush on the bed and turned back to her frowning nephew.

"Now what's the matter? Did the boys go off and leave you all alone with nothing to do? You sweet little thing! Come on, we'll go

downstairs and give you a snack." She bent
down to kiss him.

"Sweet little thing! Did she say sweet little thing?" Gordy squeaked.

"I've got it!" Nate cried. "The lever, it's
moving!" He pulled the lever down, and the
Zoomlor rose from the bed and into the air.
Mrs. Murphy had her back to Noah's bed,
but Jack gazed at the ship, wide-eyed, as it
began to gain altitude.

"No-No! No-No!" Jack cried. Mrs. Murphy shook her head, kneeling down to tie
Jack's shoe.

"Yes, yes, I know, honey. You want to
play with Noah, but he's not home. He's off
with Nate," Mrs. Murphy said. Jack
stamped his foot and turned bright red. Suddenly he remembered his monster.

"AckAck, AckAck, AckAck," he wailed.

"Where is your AckAck, honey? See if you
can find him. You can take him down to the
kitchen with you," Mrs. Murphy said.

Jack, catching sight of AckAck disappearing behind the toy chest, took off in hot pursuit. He ran to the chest and reached behind

it, pulling AckAck out by his long scaly tail.
The monster tried to wiggle free, but he
couldn't.

Jack lifted him up by his tail. As the ferocious beast hung dangling, the giggling toddler planted a kiss on his nose.

Mrs. Murphy gave AckAck a quick glance
and then looked away in disgust. "I don't
know how you can kiss that ugly thing," she
said, wincing. AckAck stuck out his tongue
at her. Everyone in the Zoomlor laughed.
Jack looked up to see the spaceship flying
around the room.

"No-No! No-No!" Jack called up to his
cousin.

"I'm sorry, you can't see Noah right now."
Mrs. Murphy tied Jack's other shoelace. But
Noah was waving from inside the Zoomlor as
it sailed over Mrs. Murphy's head and out
the bedroom door.

CHAPTER FIFTEEN

"Nate," Noah cried, "we're not in the bedroom anymore!" Everyone in the Zoomlor had been so busy looking down at Jack, they hadn't noticed that the ship had flown out of the bedroom and into the hall.

"You've got to figure out how to put her in reverse and get us back to the bedroom, Nate!" Noah yelled as they flew by the bathroom.

"Reverse? I'm not really sure where reverse is," Nate muttered, "but I'll give it a try." He pushed a silver button. They were thrown forward in their seats. Instead of backing up, the ship began to speed up. As the terrified crew looked on, the Zoomlor was flying at a frightening speed to the other end of the hallway.

"Hold on!" Nate cried, gripping the joystick. "I think I pushed the acceleration button by mistake. We're going down the stairs!" He guided them to the right and tried pushing a green button and pulling down a blue lever. Within seconds the ship returned to normal speed. Everyone breathed a sigh of relief.

"Look, there's Overdue," Noah called, pointing down to his own gigantic pet. Overdue was fast asleep on the bottom step. When he heard the soft purr of the Zoomlor's engine, he opened one eye and cocked his head.

Noah and Nate waved down to the dog, as the little purple spaceship sailed over his head. Overdue blinked several times, trying to wake up. The spaceship flew into the dining room and continued its journey through the kitchen and into the den. Jess and his piano teacher were sitting on a little bench in front of the piano.

"That's Mrs. Plumbio," Noah said, pointing to the woman below. A mass of blond bouncy curls framed the woman's oval-shaped face. Her purple triangle earrings matched the purple flowers in her dress. As she played the piano, the flowers wiggled and jiggled on her large frame. She took up most of the little bench, causing Jess to slide off every now and then.

Noah also took lessons from Mrs. Plumbio, and though he couldn't say that he really liked her, he didn't dislike her either. She was just strange. Each time a student made a mistake, she would hold her hands dramatically over her ears, wincing as if she were in pain. Noah didn't like it when she did this, but he objected more to being pushed off the bench, which is what happened when Mrs. Plumbio began playing Beethoven.

"It must be the end of the lesson," Noah said, listening to Mrs. Plumbio's shrill voice. "She always plays Beethoven at the end of the lesson, and she always says the same thing before she starts to play."

They listened as Mrs. Plumbio remarked, "Playing the piano is a creative endeavor,

Jess, and you must allow yourself to get lost in it and experience the joy of the music." Noah knew that when Mrs. Plumbio played, she would get so lost in the music that she would forget everything around her, rocking from side to side as she pounded the keys.

Mrs. Plumbio began Beethoven's Fifth Symphony. Jess was trying to stay on the bench, beside the massive pansies that were bouncing about beside him. He rolled his eyes up to the ceiling in frustration.

"Oh, wow!" Jess cried out, seeing the Zoomlor overhead. Mrs. Plumbio abruptly lifted her fingers from the keys and turned to Jess with an exasperated look. Her mouth sagged sorrowfully at the corners and then drooped down into a full-blown frown. She hated to be interrupted while she was in the middle of playing Beethoven.

"Is my playing disturbing you today, Jess?" she asked stiffly.

Jess quickly lowered his eyes to the keyboard. "Your playing? Oh, no, Mrs. Plumbio. Your playing is . . . is great . . . really great," he sputtered. Jess's sudden enthusiasm did not fool his teacher.

"I'm afraid that I'm going to have to have a word with your mother when this lesson is over, Jess," she said sternly. "You must learn to concentrate." She shook her head, her golden curls bouncing from side to side as she returned her fingers to the keys. Soon she was lost in her playing again, shifting her weight back and forth on the bench.

"Poor Jess," Noah whispered. "I bet he wishes that he had come along. It's not often that you get to ride in a spaceship that you built yourself."

"I'll turn on the deck lights for him, so he can see the ship in all her glory," Nate whispered.

"Sorry, wrong button," he croaked, as the landing gear suddenly fell down from the ship. Jess looked up just in time to see the Zoomlor's landing gear hook onto Mrs. Plumbio's golden blond curls. He sat bug-eyed as the Zoomlor lifted Mrs. Plumbio's hair from her head. Mrs. Plumbio's real hair was short and gray and still on her head, while the bouncy golden curls were airborne.

"Oh, my gosh," Noah cried, "we've stolen Mrs. Plumbio's hair!"

"It doesn't even look like she misses it," Gordy observed with a giggle. It was true. Mrs. Plumbio went right on pounding the keys in a fury of inspiration. She rocked from side to side and bobbed her head wildly, so that she never even noticed that her wig was floating above her. Jess, meanwhile, was perched on a small corner of the bench, his mouth open and his eyes as round as doorknobs.

"Nate, do something!" Noah exclaimed.

"I'm trying to figure out how to get the landing gear back up," Nate told him.

"Don't do that!" Noah cried. "If the landing gear comes back up, Mrs. Plumbio's hair will come up with it."

"Maybe by activating the landing gear, we can shake the wig loose," the Commander suggested. Nate put the ship in a holding pattern just above Mrs. Plumbio's head. Then he set to work on reactivating the landing

gear. Noah, meanwhile, looked down to see Overdue below. He had come into the room and was sitting on the floor next to the piano bench. He cocked his head and whimpered as he gazed up at the spaceship.

"OK, we're ready to take her up," Nate whispered. Everyone watched as the wig slowly rose in the air along with the landing gear. But the golden curls suddenly came loose and fell from the ship. Mrs. Plumbio was bouncing back and forth so much that the wig missed her head, landing on Over-due instead! A mass of curly blond ringlets framed his furry brown face.

In a bold move, Jess pulled the wig off Overdue and stretched to place it back on Mrs. Plumbio's head. She was so involved in her playing that she never even noticed.

Mrs. Plumbio lifted her hands from the keys, her face flushed with the excitement of the creative experience. Her eyes shone with the joy of the music, and her wig sat backward on the top of her head.

CHAPTER SIXTEEN

As Mrs. Plumbio was lecturing Jess on his poor concentration, the Zoomlor was flying out of the room. It sailed through the hall and into the kitchen.

Mr. Murphy was looking in the refrigerator for a snack, while Mrs. Murphy was standing at the sink, washing dishes. Jack was in his high chair having a piece of carrot cake and some milk, with AckAck beside him. The ugly monster was wearing a little flowery doll's bib around his neck. His long lizardlike tongue curled its way into Jack's cup, quietly lapping up some milk.

Nate guided the ship up and over the top

of the cabinets. Noah looked down to see Mrs. Plumbio suddenly standing in the doorway. She had come into the room to speak to Mrs. Murphy about Jess's poor concentration. Mrs. Plumbio was totally unaware of how ridiculous she looked, standing there so straight and serious, with her wig on backward. She opened her mouth to speak, when AckAck suddenly burped. It was a loud, growly sort of monster burp.

"Are you all right, Mrs. Plumbio?" Mr. Murphy managed to sputter as he grabbed his side with laughter. Without another word, Mrs. Plumbio turned around and left the house, too angry to say good-bye, much less give her lecture on Jess.

Now everyone in the kitchen was giggling. Only AckAck was quiet as he sat silently licking the icing from Jack's carrot cake. Suddenly the monster heard the soft purr of the Zoomlor's engines. He tilted his head and twisted his neck, stretching it as far as he could in the direction of the cabinets. Jack followed AckAck's gaze and let out a happy whoop at the sight of the Zoomlor.

Mr. Murphy turned around just in time to see Jack about to hurl his cup in the air.

"No, Jack!" Mr. Murphy called, coming over to the high chair. "That's not a football. It is a cup and we do not throw cups," he said sternly, taking the cup from Jack's hand. "I think he wants more milk," Mr. Murphy said, looking over at his wife.

"I just filled that cup! He certainly is thirsty," Mrs. Murphy exclaimed. "Would you refill it, dear, while I finish washing these dishes?" She turned back to the sink. Mr. Murphy opened the refrigerator. The Zoomlor sailed down from the cabinets, hovering for a few seconds over the high chair.

The crew waved to Jack and his monster. Gordy was leaning over so far in his seat that he accidentally fell on a small silver button on the instrument panel. Suddenly a ray of white light shot out from one of the laser guns and zapped the piece of carrot cake from which AckAck was about to take a bite. The cake was instantly vaporized. All that remained was a tiny puff of smoke.

"Oooooo . . ." Jack cooed, clapping his

chubby little hands. The startled monster wiggled his tongue in the air, trying to eat the smoke, but it didn't taste at all like carrot cake. He growled angrily, stretching his neck as he tried to nip at the Zoomlor, idling just inches above him.

Noah turned to Gordy and grinned. "Nice shooting."

"Aw, don't mention it." Gordy blushed, but everyone knew that he was proud of himself.

"I forgot all about the laser guns," Noah admitted, somewhat embarrassed.

"We could have used them when AckAck was attacking," Nate said, guiding the ship across the kitchen. Everyone turned in his seat to look back at the disgruntled monster, who was still trying to lick up the carrot cake smoke.

"I don't know," the Commander smiled. "I think we did just fine with marbles and catapults." They sailed out of the kitchen and into the hall.

"So what will our new destination be?" Nate asked.

"We'd better go back to my bedroom and see how the General and Crunch are doing," Noah told him.

Nate nodded and steered them back up the stairs.

"Where is everybody?" Noah wondered aloud as they flew into his bedroom.

"I don't know," Nate replied. "Let's take a look around." The Zoomlor slowly circled the room, flying close to the floor. As Nate steered it around the bend at the end of the bed, it ran into a cloud of glitter. Gold and silver sparkles rained down on the ship as Nate brought it in for a landing on the launchpad. Noah looked up to see the space station before them. It was suddenly lit from top to bottom in a dazzle of colored lights, restored to its original splendor.

"It looks like the army men and the wrestlers have been busy cleaning up the mess that AckAck made," the Commander said, noticing that the catapults were back in place. The little pink wrestlers and olive-green army men were cheering wildly from the walkways of the station. The army men were manning the catapults and had filled them with glitter.

As the crew from the Zoomlor stepped out of the ship and made its way down the ramp, the army men stationed at the catapults steadied their aim. They released the firing mechanisms, and a shower of golden glitter fell down on the returning heroes. Cheers and whistles filled the air as hundreds of wrestlers and army men waved their arms above their heads.

"I guess this brings us to the end of our adventure," the Commander said, turning to Noah.

"Already?" Noah frowned.

The Commander placed his hand on Noah's shoulder and smiled. "I'm proud of you, Noah. You really took charge of things. You faced your fears head-on. We came through this adventure with flying colors. Now I think that you'd better say a few words to your fans. They've probably been worried about you." The Commander pointed to the crowds gathered on the walkways. Noah waved.

"I . . . I don't know what to say," Noah stammered, "except thank you, thank all of you," he called out to them. "Crunch, you and your men gave us the muscle we needed." The wrestlers went wild with applause. Crunch joined them in forming a spontaneous pyramid. "And General Meatball, you and your troops acted with bravery and honor," Noah continued. The General led his men in a cheer and a salute. "This is one adventure I know I'll never forget." The crowd roared, and the room was filled with the clapping of hundreds of little pink and green hands.

Noah looked over to see the Commander motioning to him. "I think it's time to go," the Commander whispered in Noah's ear. "We'd better get you and Nate away from the space station before you return to normal size, or you could do more damage than AckAck. Gordy and I will escort you as far as the rock wall."

Noah felt a little dizzy. He realized that the magic must be wearing off. He reluctantly made his way with Nate, the Commander, and Gordy toward the rock tunnel.

It's almost over, Noah was thinking. The best adventure of my life is almost over. No one spoke, as they made their way through the tunnel. When they had almost reached the other side, the Commander suddenly stopped.

"We'll have to say our good-byes here," he said softly.

Gordy turned to Nate and flashed his gap-toothed grin. "You sure fly a mean machine, Captain," he said.

"And you sure do shoot a mean laser gun, Sergeant." Gordy reached over to tousle his hair. Then Gordy's face grew serious and he turned to Noah.

"Noah, before you go," he whispered, "could you promise me something?"

"Sure, Gordy, what is it?" Noah asked.

"Could you promise that you won't send me on any more oatmeal missions? They're the worst, you know." Gordy winced.

"I promise." Noah laughed. "No more oatmeal. You deserve better than that. With all your training and skill, you're ready for advancement. Next time it will be a mashed potato mission for sure." Noah winked, then turned to the Commander.

"I never did get to tell you how much I admire you," Noah said shyly. "I guess you're kind of like a hero to me, and I wish that we had more time together." He tried hard to hold back his tears.

The Commander reached out and put his arms around him. "I've never been very good at good-byes myself," the Commander said softly. "But this isn't forever, you know. There is still some magic powder left, isn't there?"

"Yes, I told Jess to put it in a safe place," Noah said, his face brightening. "We can have another adventure, can't we, Commander?"

The Commander smiled. "I look forward to it, old friend," he said, giving Noah one last hug. Then he and Gordy turned around and began walking back toward the space station. Noah watched the two figures disappearing down the tunnel.

"I'm going to miss you, old friend. I'm

really going to miss you," Noah whispered.

"We'd better get going," Nate said. He grabbed Noah's arm. As the two began to run, they heard Gordy's goofy voice echoing through the tunnel.

"And don't forget to come back soon," he called. "I never did get to hear about the meatless meat loaf."

Noah looked at Nate and the two broke out laughing. "We'll be back soon, Gordy!" Noah shouted. "And we'll tell you about the meat loaf. We'll be back . . . I promise, we'll be back. . . ."